TEEN-AGE
SPORTS PARADE

The Teen-Age Library

TEEN-AGE STORIES OF ACTION
Edited by Frank Owen

TEEN-AGE ADVENTURE STORIES
By Charles I. Coombs

TEEN-AGE AVIATION STORIES
Edited by Don Samson

TEEN-AGE BASEBALL STORIES
Edited by Frank Owen

TEEN-AGE BOY SCOUT STORIES
By Irving Crump

TEEN-AGE COMPANION
Edited by Frank Owen

TEEN-AGE FOOTBALL STORIES
Edited by Frank Owen

TEEN-AGE HISTORICAL STORIES
By Russell Gordon Carter

TEEN-AGE MYSTERY STORIES
Edited by Frank Owen

TEEN-AGE OUTDOOR STORIES
Edited by Frank Owen

TEEN-AGE SEA STORIES
Edited by David Thomas

TEEN-AGE SPORTS STORIES
Edited by Frank Owen

TEEN-AGE TREASURE CHEST OF SPORTS STORIES
By Charles I. Coombs

TEEN-AGE STORIES OF THE WEST
By Stephen Payne

TEEN-AGE WINTER SPORTS STORIES
Edited by Frank Owen

TEEN-AGE ANIMAL STORIES
By Russell Gordon Carter

TEEN-AGE COWBOY STORIES
By Stephen Payne

TEEN-AGE BASKETBALL STORIES
By Josh Furman

TEEN-AGE DOG STORIES
Edited by David Thomas

TEEN-AGE SPORTS PARADE
By B. J. Chute

TEEN-AGE
SPORTS
PARADE

By

B. J. CHUTE

Illustrated by William B. Ricketts

Grosset & Dunlap *Publishers*
NEW YORK

For my nephew, Bill

Contents

It wasn't exactly on the palatial side—comfortable enough, but the furniture was shabby and the second bed was obviously an extra.

"Kind of small, isn't it?" said Chad, answering the look. "I've cleared out half the closet, so if you're good at condensing we'll get along all right. You can have either bed. One squeaks, and one has a baby mountain in the middle of it."

"I'll take the squeak." Ty settled for comfort, and Chad nodded casually. Ty slung his suitcases onto the cot and began to unpack, while Chad straddled a chair and watched with interest. After a moment, Ty said curiously, "What kind of dump is this, anyway?"

"Dump?"

"The school, I mean. Sorry. It's pretty small compared to the one I transferred from. Got a swimming pool, for instance?"

"Not yet. We've only just finished paying for the football field."

Ty gave him a quick glance. "You on the team?"

"M'hm. Left half."

One of Ty's eyebrows traveled up. "That's my spot. I hope you don't mind competition." Without waiting for an answer, he dug into his suitcase and dragged out a fat, looseleaf notebook that he tossed to Chad.

Chad opened it, riffled through the pages and gave a low whistle. "Press clippings, huh? Looks like you're pretty good at your job."

"I'm good," said Ty briefly, and took the book back.

"The firm of Evans and Evans," said Chad, "welcomes competition. But there may be an opening at tackle. Could I interest you?"

Ty gave a short laugh. "Me? What do you think I am—a truck horse? No, thanks." He pulled a jacket out of his suitcase and gave it a shake. "Where's the coat hanger?"

Chad didn't answer for a moment. Then he got up and crossed the room to the closet. "There aren't any extras. You can use a couple of mine till you get your own."

The coach was short and stocky, with a bald head that evaded the sun under a tacky baseball cap. Ty, looking him over, decided that he probably knew his job.

The teams lined up. Ty's glance went automatically to Chad in the varsity backfield. He was standing limp with his hands hanging at his sides and his eyes check-ing the field of play. Another guy who probably knew his job, Ty decided reluctantly.

The whistle blew, and the center snapped the ball to the fullback who faked a pass to right half, then

Ty gave a short laugh. "Me? What do you think I am—a truck horse? No, thanks." He pulled a jacket out of his suitcase and gave it a shake. "Where's the coat hangers?"

Chad didn't answer for a moment. Then he got up and crossed the room to the closet. "There aren't any extras. You can use a couple of mine till you get your own."

"O.K.," said Ty easily. "That'll do."

The football field was a neat job of work, its green turf springy and cleanly marked, its tiers of bleachers ample for a big crowd. Warm fall sunshine struck golden on the players' helmets and glinted against the water pail. Ty, standing on the sidelines, shrugged his coat off his shoulders and draped it over one arm, not taking his eyes off the field.

The varsity was walking through a complicated half-spinner play with methodical accuracy, checking assignments. Coach Bradley nodded satisfaction and blew his whistle. "O.K., boys, we'll take it now." He grinned at his second team. "Mess it up for them."

The coach was short and stocky, with a bald head that evaded the sun under a tacky baseball cap. Ty, looking him over, decided that he probably knew his job.

The teams lined up. Ty's glance went automatically to Chad in the varsity backfield. He was standing limp with his hands hanging at his sides and his eyes checking the field of play. Another guy who probably knew his job, Ty decided reluctantly.

The whistle blew, and the center snapped the ball to the fullback who faked a pass to right half, then

Ty said stiffly, "Left half's my position."

"O.K." The coach shrugged, then gestured toward a dark-haired second stringer. "Go in at Mason's place, Ty, and show us what you can do."

Ty nodded. Chad, dropping back into defensive position, grinned and sketched a salute of welcome. The second team went into a huddle and came out of it fast on their own forty-yard line. There was nothing fancy about the play. The ball went to Ty on an end run. The pass from center was soft and nice to handle. Ty pulled the ball in against his chest, the old feeling of excited assurance welling up inside him.

The second-string blocking was devoted but not impressive, and the hard-charging varsity line was murder on cleats. It was speed that got Ty over the midfield stripe, it was split-second guessing that got him over the varsity's forty-five, and it was a pattern of pivots and sidestepping that got him past the clutching fingers of the secondary and into the open, before two men teamed up to poleaxe him on the varsity thirty-three.

Ty got to his feet, cradling the ball, and shook himself like a water spaniel, then looked quickly toward Coach Bradley. The coach had a speculative look in his mild blue eyes, and Ty felt a tug of satisfaction. Tackle, huh? Not for this baby.

The second team crowded around him, chortling audibly, and the varsity captain and quarterback, Kenny Simons, said "M'mm, special delivery" admiringly. Chad said, "Very nifty," sounding a little surprised. Ty grinned.

The coach said briefly, "Stay in at half for the afternoon, Ty. You seem to have something there."

There weren't any more fireworks. The varsity line saw to that and snarled the second-string blocking up unmercifully. But, whenever Ty could shake loose, he proved that he carried dynamite to spare, and his weaving hips, fast footwork and bombsight passing made plenty of trouble for the tougher team.

In the locker room, afterwards, he was the center of attention. Leaning against the wall with a towel slung over his shoulder, he told them about his career at Alister. All-Conference in the county league, mentioned for All-State, key man on a winning eleven that had swept the field in all its games.

"They'll miss you," a second-string player remarked admiringly.

Ty nodded. "My father's business moved him more than halfway across the country," he explained. "Utilities." He stretched and yawned, then picked up his discarded football shoes from the bench, looked them over and yelled for the manager. "Hey, bud! What's the big idea, giving me an old pair?"

The manager, counting jerseys, straightened up, looked at Ty for a moment, then shrugged. "I'll see what I can do," he said, amiably enough. "You've got big feet."

"The better to kick with, my dear," said Ty with just a touch too much sweetness. "I can dropkick that little ball from just about anywhere on the field."

Kenny Simons grinned. "Modest little violet, aren't you?"

Ty grinned back, undisturbed. "Why not? I've got the goods."

"Well," said Kenny slowly, "maybe you're right."

a blackboard and carried to the field. But he raged inwardly against the slowness of a line that allowed him only yardage on plays that ought to score. Any one of those plays, sparkplugged by himself on the varsity, would have been streamlined homicide. Instead, they'd start big, then he'd get held up by his own interference and, brilliant as he was, he'd be caught.

He went back into the lineup for a double fake reverse and run that had scored for Caldwell against a powerful Lincoln eleven. It was monkey business. Very nice monkey business, guaranteed to stand the gallery's hair on end.

The ball went to Ty, cuddling into his waiting hands. He faked to the fullback, then reversed and faked beautifully to Slats. Slats cooperated, and Ty had the varsity playing hide-and-seek for a split second before they tagged the ball. A split second was all that Ty ever needed.

He blazed off around end and broke for the sidelines. A varsity man threw a grass-cutting tackle at him. Ty sideslipped, barely escaped stepping out of bounds, and cut back to safer territory. Safer territory was full of tacklers. Ty checked, pivoted and swiveled through with the width of a coat of paint between him and a permanent stop.

Feet pounding and head down, he streaked for the goal. Kenny Simons was waiting for him at safety, and Kenny might be small but he was scrappy. Ty charged straight at him, then, as Kenny dived, he stopped on a dime, whirled and did a fadeaway. Kenny stopped a handful of clovers from crossing the goal line, but he didn't stop Ty.

Ty stepped over the stripe and planted the ball in the end zone.

Coach Bradley dismissed them early that afternoon and Ty hung around the field, rather expecting to be called to the coach's side. When nothing happened and the stocky mentor went on placidly giving some tips on pass-handling to an end, Ty shrugged and followed the others off the gridiron.

He dressed fast and managed to catch up with Kenny Simons outside. He wanted private conversation with the varsity captain, and luck was with him. Kenny was heading for an appointment with a Mr. William Shakespeare. Ty fell into step.

"How'd you like that play?" Ty inquired.

"Very purty," said Kenny, not needing to ask which play Ty meant.

"I didn't get much help from the line, of course," Ty observed casually. "With you guys, I can really go to town."

"Ummm," said Kenny in a conversational outburst.

Ty gave him a faintly resentful look. That was where Kenny should have said something definite. He decided the kid-glove approach was wasted, so he said right out, "When do you think Bradley will put me on the varsity?"

There was a long silence, so long that Ty thought he wasn't going to get an answer. Then Kenny said slowly, "Take it easy, Ty. We've got a pretty strong backfield combination with Chad in. We're doing all right."

Ty said, "Chad's not in my class."

Kenny shot a quick look at him. "He's quite a ball player, and we work together well. The coach likes Chad's game."

"The coach," said Ty flatly, "likes Chad."

"That's a quaint remark."

Ty blazed up. "What's quaint about it? You've got a nice little closed corporation there, and I'm an outsider. Chad's got a three-year in, and your friend Bradley is the cautious type. Chad's playing that angle very neatly."

"Chad doesn't play angles," Kenny snapped, responding to the temper in Ty's voice. "And the coach is running the team. You're rushing your fences, Henderson."

So Kenny liked Chad too. Just a bunch of pals. Ty checked a sharp retort, because there wasn't any percentage in antagonizing the captain. "Ease off," he said. "I just had a notion you guys liked touchdowns."

They stopped at the foot of the library steps and looked at each other. Then Kenny said again, "The coach is running the team," turned and left him.

Ty watched him go. He'd been right in his guess. Chad was the white-haired boy around this bunch— three years' seniority and a nice dependable halfback. It was going to take dynamite to dislodge him.

Well, if Henderson wasn't dynamite, who was? He spun on his heel and headed for King Hall.

He found Chad lying on the bed, reading a history book upside down. When Ty came into the room, Chad dropped his book and sat up. "I've been waiting for you," he said.

you'd like to know." He picked up his book again, pointedly ending the conversation.

For a little while, Ty just went on staring. Then incredulity was replaced with a violent surge of pleasure. Visions of newspaper headlines danced in front of his eyes. Ty Henderson Brilliant in Marshall Victory. Ty Henderson Scores Winning Touchdown. Ty Henderson—

Within two weeks, he was making those headlines come true. The Marshall cheering section had a new chant now. "Give the ball to Ty." They responded wildly to the special excitement of his brand of playing, and whenever he laid hands on the leather they went mad.

Sometimes Ty thought Kenny was too darned cautious about calling his signals, relying too much on line play. Once, in the locker room, he said as much, and it turned out to be a mistake. Kenny crawled right down his throat, and a couple of his teammates backed him up. Ty let it drop. It was natural for them to see green a bit. Before he'd turned up, the fans had known there were four men in the Marshall backfield. Now they could only see one.

The occasional flare-ups didn't bother him much, although he had moments of wishing he was more one of the gang. Chad still seemed to keep the same relationship with the others, even now when he was sweating it out on the second string.

But it didn't matter. Things were going O.K. He bought a new notebook for press clippings, and he was a campus hero.

Then Marshall dropped a game.

The Farwell team had an unimpressive record but a front wall made of concrete. Their schedule had given them an open date the week before, while Marshall had barely grabbed a tough decision, and the Marshall line, showing signs of reaction, broke against Farwell's stone wall and receded like waves against a dike.

They came into the fourth quarter six points in the hole, after a brutal downfield march had carried the big Farwell eleven over the goal line.

The Marshall stands had been selling their wares: "Give the ball to Ty. Give the ball to Ty." And then, when Ty got tied up, they quit asking. He raged hopelessly as his interference bogged down, and there was real tension in a time-out. Farwell had held for downs, and, angry and derisive at his teammates because they couldn't shake their star back loose, Ty made a crack about paperweight champions.

Hugh Lawrence at right guard took him up on it. "I don't notice you breaking your neck on defense," he snapped. "You've muffed a couple of tackles in the secondary this afternoon, pal."

Ty didn't like criticism. He opened his mouth for a retort, and Pete Holmes cut in. "Dry up," said Pete, meaning it. The big, easy-going fullback wasn't much for speaking his piece, but when he did it stayed spoke. Ty and Hugh dried up simultaneously.

And, finally, with less than a minute to go Ty got his chance. It came on a wide lateral, and his interference opened up daylight. Ty checked the field, his mind recording the play like a camera. Two Farwell men were coming in, and once he had split through his chink of light he would have to cope with them.

run. Seventeen yards picked up by dogged persistence and the help of a line that was paying attention. Chad was working hard these days.

Ty shrugged. It would take more than hard work if Chad intended to carry out his threat to get the varsity post back. Ty knew that, if he himself had been lugging the pigskin on that play, the guard wouldn't have caught him. A quick feint would have taken him right around Hugh Lawrence. Hugh had a bad habit of planting himself just before he dived, and a really smart runner could throw him off balance. But not Chad.

Just the same, the second team had a first down in varsity territory. They came up fast on the scrimmage line, and the ball went to the fullback. Ty was watching Chad, expecting him to carry the ball again. After all, what Chad was aiming for was to build himself up in the coach's eyes. He wouldn't even need to tip off Danny Cleves, the second-string quarterback. Danny would know who was top man on the second team.

Instead, the ball went to Slats Jameson, and Chad teamed with the tackle and guard who pulled out of the line to form Slats' interference. Chad took out the varsity right end with a roll-block that meant business.

Ty, watching Chad, was slow coming in, and Slats had plenty of time to whip the ball to his own right end. The left end's decoy wasn't too hot, and the varsity caught the ball carrier and mowed him down in his tracks, but the second string had picked up yardage again.

Kenny Simons, crossing over in front of Ty, said sharply, "Have a nice daydream?" Ty muttered a savage retort, but the next time the play came his way the ball carrier was nailed. "How does that suit your Royal Highness?" Ty inquired elaborately, and got a blank look for his pains.

Chad's gang lost the ball on downs, and Ty joined the huddle confidently. He only needed to put his own hands on the leather to show Chad who was the real halfback on the field. His luck, however, was out. The coach's whistle ended scrimmage for the afternoon.

Ty started a slow jog around the field. Chad had stopped to show Slats something about a shoulder block, and Ty slowed down curiously. Slats always had trouble coming in under a straightarm and it made him an easy man to take out.

"Look," said Chad, demonstrating. "You've got to come under and up if you want to stop me. Tunnel, don't shove." Slats grinned and said it was more fun shoving, but, amiably, he tried Chad's suggestion. It worked, and the two players rolled on the turf.

"Pal," said Slats reverently, "you've got something there. Let's try it again."

Ty looked at them both for a moment, then shrugged his shoulders and started off again, registering the reflection that Chad was a dope. Taking blocks like that was a good way to wear yourself out.

He finished his tour of the field and headed for the lockers, frowning a little. Chad on the second team had made more yardage that afternoon than Ty on the first, and it didn't add up. The varsity hadn't been clicking any too well lately, and it was hard to put a finger on what was wrong. Everybody seemed edgy.

In the locker room, it showed up even more than on

Kenny reached for his shirt. "Medium soft, I think. Treanor hasn't got much to show except a guy named Malone. One-man team, I hear."

"Andy Malone? I read about him in the News the other day."

"He's really hot."

"Him?" Ty dismissed the competition easily. "I'll run rings around that guy."

Kenny gave him a quick glance, then shrugged and pulled his shirt on over his head.

Little Treanor Prep turned out to have the will to deliver, but not the goods. Their line from end to end was bendable, and Marshall bent it. Early in the first quarter, Ty fielded a kick on his own forty and ran it back for an easy touchdown over a field that sprawled with Treanor men, blasted out of the play by the Marshall front wall.

On their next series of downs, Marshall plowed through again and brought the ball straight back to the enemy seventeen. In the huddle, Ty said, "I'll take it around end."

Kenny said shortly, "Pete'll handle this. Three bucks and we'll be over."

Marshall's star ball player didn't like the idea and said so. "I can take it across in one on an end run," he objected. "What's the sense—"

Kenny looked at him. "I'll call the plays, Ty."

Most of the others backed Kenny, but a few sided with Ty who said angrily, "There wasn't anything wrong with that last touchdown I made, was there?"

"You waltzed down an open field," Kenny reminded him. "And I'll call the plays. *If* you please."

He didn't please, but the majority ruled. Angry, Ty walked back into position. It took Pete only two plays, instead of three, to make good on his assignment, and the approval from the grandstand was for the fullback. Ty asked himself furiously what was the good of a triple-threat ace if you used him like a workhorse. With him on the ball, they could score on the flashy runs that the crowd really loved, opening the game up wide.

Off-tackle slants. Power plays. Kenny was a sucker for that stuff.

Or was he? Wasn't Kenny perhaps a little on the green-eyed side? Wasn't he a little sore at the idea of Ty Henderson collecting the medals?

In the huddle again, there was another argument. Choo-Choo got the nod to convert and, although he made it good, the ball nearly angled off the crossbar. With Ty's boot behind it, it would have been centered dead to rights.

"Some quarterback!" Ty muttered. "Taking a chance on scores!" The left tackle nodded sympathetically.

Kenny, seeing the exchange, gave them both a sharp look. And, after that, he mixed the plays more than ever, with everybody in the backfield getting a whack at the ball, with the ends pass-catching, and even Kenny himself producing a showy quick kick.

The system, if you were watching from the grandstand, worked. Marshall's powerhouse ran up a good score by the end of the half. But why wouldn't it work? The Treanor line was cream puff. You could give the ball to a puppy, and he'd score too.

Ty spoke his piece a couple of times, and the friction

Tommy Kraft at left end got into the fight unexpectedly. Tommy thought Ty was tops. "Quit riding him," he said. "Everybody misses them occasionally."

It was third down and still, stupidly, eight yards to go. Kenny, tight-mouthed, called a kick.

And a Treanor man popped up out of the clovers and blocked it.

"Great stuff," said Ty witheringly.

He said it again, a moment later, when Treanor's Andy Malone took a razzle-dazzle chance and sailed a whizzer over the heads of the Marshall team, completing an elegant long pass in the Marshall end zone.

That made it Marshall, 27; Treanor, 6. And Coach Bradley sent in the whole second team.

They looked—and Ty on the bench didn't like it—plenty good. They had snap and polish and some football savvy they hadn't had a couple of weeks ago. It was playing against a weak line, of course, that showed it off, but just the same something inside Ty stiffened. Chad looked really expert. You could sit there on the bench and know that any good runner behind a medium-strong line and medium-good blocking would look all right. You could sit there and remember how easy it was to streak down a field when the opposition was flat on its face. You could dig up a lot of explanations, and they'd be the right ones. But you still couldn't argue with the fact that Chad looked good.

. . . "I'm going to get your job away from you, Henderson." . . .

And today it was Evans who was making the showing, and Henderson who was watching. What was happening? What was going wrong? He couldn't get it. It didn't make sense.

Way deep down, Ty began to get scared.

The editor of the Weekly said that the Marshall varsity was stale, and he wrote a mournful article on the subject. The team, he said, had passed its peak too early in the season, and he took an accordingly dim view of the Ridgewood game.

Ty would have liked to think he was right. It was an easy out. But it also wasn't true. It wasn't the varsity's staleness that accented the snap in the second team's playing. It was something else.

It was, for instance, the way the second team ran through drills. It was the way they were on the ball like steel traps, the way they worked together like veterans.

The tighter the second string pulled, the looser-knit the varsity looked. The line wasn't shaking Ty loose, the backfield wasn't giving him the kind of blocking he had the right to expect. The old feeling of confidence he had when he laid hands on leather wasn't with him any more. He'd be slammed down by a tackle and get up raging at the guy who should have led him through the play. And, even if nothing was said, tension hung in the air as thick as a harbor fog. Kenny threw fewer and fewer plays his way in scrimmage, discriminating against him. Even easy-going Choo-Choo got snappish, and once an argument on the field came close to ending in a fist fight.

The second team stayed cool. In their huddles, they had their arms around each other's shoulders. The line kidded the backfield and blasted big holes for them. The backfield elaborately mourned the inefficiency of the line and then piled up yardage behind it. In the locker room, nobody but the second stringers had fun.

Ty couldn't figure it. There wasn't any reason why the better team should be looking bad. The varsity was pulling in all directions, and tempers were as scratchy as wildcats.

And then, a few days before the Ridgewood game, in a scrimmage, Chad scored a touchdown on the varsity. U. S. 752063

There weren't any fireworks—just straight ball handling, smashing blocks and a hole that opened up. And Ty at safety was too slow, like the rest of his teammates, to realize what had happened and to stop it. Chad didn't feint around Ty. He went through and over him like a tank. Ty's mind had been on one of Kenny's inevitable cracks, he wasn't paying attention, he wasn't coordinating. You could write it off as a lucky break for Chad, but it still added up neatly to a second-string score.

Ty picked himself off the ground, aching from the jolt of Chad's muscular body cracking into his, and the first thing he did was to look quick to see if the coach had been watching. Bradley had, of course. Trust old Seeing-Eye Bradley.

The coach's face was very thoughtful for a moment, then he nodded to himself. And, about three minutes later, he called Chad over to his side.

Ty walked back to King Hall with a set of mixed-up emotions. He didn't need a crystal ball to tell him what the coach had said to Chad. Chad was in; Ty was out. Period.

And what the blazes difference did it make now? Ty thought savagely. There weren't going to be any headlines for any halfback on the Marshall varsity, the way they were playing now. The team was shot. Why kid himself? Something had gone wrong somewhere, and a bunch of guys who had looked good early in the season were just another ragged has-been team now.

Let Chad play behind that line! Who cared, any more?

He wrenched open the door of their room. Chad was standing by his desk, and he turned around quickly at the sound of Ty's entrance. He said, "I've been waiting for you, Ty. You and me are going to have a talk."

"Save your breath," Ty said. "I know you've got the varsity job back again. Well, you're welcome to it." He crossed to the window, yanked the curtain back and stood for a moment, staring blindly down at the campus. All his dreams of glory had gone up in smoke. He was licked. Just because ten other guys wouldn't give him the support a star player deserved. How could he look good? Could one player fill every pair of shoes on the team?

Chad, behind him, said, "Sit down a minute, Ty."

Ty said angrily, "I'll stand." The room was half his. The chairs were half his. He'd do as he pleased.

"Suit yourself." There was a moment's silence.

After a while, Ty turned around. Chad had dropped into a chair and was leaning forward with his elbows on his knees, his hands clasped. Ty said, "Well?" belligerently.

Chad said slowly, "I thought I did the right thing when I got off the team to make way for you. I didn't. I'd have done better to have stayed." He looked at the carpet. "You've managed to wreck a swell ball team, Ty."

Ty stared. "*I* wrecked them?" He gave a short laugh. "Who do you think you're kidding?"

"I'm not kidding anybody," Chad said matter-of-factly. "Not even myself any more. I figured you were a great halfback. So I got out. It was the dumbest thing I ever did in my life." He looked up. "You're no football player, Ty."

Chad meant what he was saying, crazy as it sounded. Ty said, "I don't get it."

"I know you don't," Chad agreed. "But you would if you thought about it. Anybody on the squad could tell you."

"Okay, so I'm dumb."

Chad looked down at his hands, then up at Ty again. "Can't you honestly see what's happened to the varsity, Ty?"

"Sure. They've laid down on the job."

Chad's shoulders moved impatiently.

"Well? Haven't they?"

"No. You're the guy who's laid down." He went on without giving Ty a chance to interrupt. "When you came, everyone said it was a break for Marshall. The coach and the team and I—we all figured we'd got a really big-time player. We thought we'd go places. What we didn't count on was that you couldn't play as a member of a team at all. You could only play as Ty Henderson."

Ty said accusingly, "That's an easy out for you, isn't it?"

"Not particularly. Do a little thinking, Ty. Which is better now—the varsity or the second string?"

Ty hesitated. "The second string," he admitted reluctantly.

"Why?"

"*I* don't know." He jammed his hands into his pockets. "What are you driving at?"

"The second string's better because they're playing as a team. At the moment, I'm better than you are at half, because I'm playing *with* my bunch. We've been pulling together while, thanks to you, the varsity's been pulling apart. When I'm running the ball, I'm one guy in eleven doing a job. When you run it, you think you're the whole team. You don't see why anyone else should share the spotlight. You don't want the team as a team. You want the team as a background for yourself." His voice sharpened. "Well, you've got it, brother. How do you like it now?"

Ty looked at the floor. He knew the answer to that one. What he had now was nothing. A nice round zero.

And then, suddenly, he was angry. He lashed out. "O.K. Maybe I was wrong. I'll admit it. But what's the good of telling me all this now, when it's too late? You've got the job back, and I suppose now you think all you have to do is cooperate all over the place and dash right out and beat Ridgewood. I suppose you figure that with you on the team—"

"Save it," said Chad. "I don't figure anything. That's why I wanted to talk to you. You're still the best halfback Marshall ever saw."

Ty stared at him.

Chad said, "With me back on the team, we still couldn't beat Ridgewood. Oh, maybe we'd play better ball—in fact, we would—but not that much better. But with you in— You've seen what cooperation can do, even on a second team. If you'd work with those varsity guys, Ty, really play football—" He smacked his fist into the palm of his hand. "We'd have a chance then. We'd have at least a halfway chance."

Ty's heart gave a sudden lurch and began to beat fast. "You mean—"

"I mean that I'm willing to get out of your way again. I mean that you can stay on the varsity. *If* you'll cut the grandstanding and really get down to work. If you'll give those guys the break they've always been willing to give you."

It didn't take Ty a quarter of a second to know the answer to that one. Work? He'd work his head off. He'd cooperate until he was purple in the face. He'd lead that Marshall team to a victory that would go down in history. He'd really give the sports columnists something to talk about. He'd show them all.

Chad said, "Well?"

Ty drew a deep breath. "I'll do it," he said. "All the way."

"If you'll even try, Ty." Chad got to his feet. "There isn't very much time, and Ridgewood's plenty tough."

Ty looked at him, suddenly realizing just how little time there was. Ridgewood was tough all right, a team that was clicking. On paper now, they'd tear Marshall to bits. Maybe it was too late, after all.

For a second, he had to fight off a feeling of real panic.

Marshall had to win. They *had* to.

III.

Ty stood on the edge of the football field, before practice the next afternoon, and looked around him, frowning worriedly.

A guy couldn't just start running all over the place, clapping his hands and shouting, "Look, fellows, I'm cooperating." And this idea of building up the other player was something new in his books, especially when there was so little time before the Ridgewood game.

Kenny Simons was parked doggedly at the twenty-yard line with a football in his hands and a deep crease between his eyebrows. As Ty watched, he held the ball out, dropped it and caught it on his boot. The kick was long and high enough but angled too much. The leather struck the crossbar and shot off sideways.

Kenny muttered something uncomplimentary about himself under his breath, stalked off to get the ball and patiently returned to his original position.

Ty crossed to his side. "You're slicing it, Kenny," he said.

Kenny gave him a look. It was a look that Ty had gotten used to the last few weeks, and it meant "play on your own side of the fence." But it was the first time he'd had to push down a feeling of resentment. This wasn't the time or the place for feeling any more. He was keeping his mind on that Ridgewood game.

He said pleasantly, "You aren't pulling both hands

away together, Kenny. Your left hand's slow, and you get a crooked bounce."

Kenny's jaw dropped.

"Here. Let me show you." He had never shared his football knowledge with another player before, and it seemed funny, but he took the ball firmly out of Kenny's hands and dropkicked it. It hopped over the crossbar like a California jackrabbit. "See what I mean?" Ty said over his shoulder as he went to retrieve it. "Both hands off the ball at exactly the same time. Try it."

"I—" said Kenny, then shook his head in bewilderment and gripped the leather. He was a smart athlete, and he caught on quick. This time the kick cut the crossbar exactly in half.

"Nice going," said Ty appreciatively.

There was a moment's silence. Then Kenny said, "Well, thanks," in a rather stunned voice.

"Any time," Ty said amiably, and walked away.

Scrimmage started a few minutes later, and Ty firmly continued his program of morale-building. When Choo-Choo threw a competent block, Ty gave him a light whack on the shoulder and said, "Atta kid." Choo-Choo's eyebrows went up like an elevator, but he grinned in acknowledgment.

Ty dropped back to kick, feeling rather pleased with himself. Chad had exaggerated the varsity's frame of mind. A little soft-soap did wonders. They'd be working with him again in practically no time. Gangway, Ridgewood!

His hands reached automatically for the pass, fingers curled knowingly along the ball's laces, and he punted a getaway kick.

It came within an inch of being blocked.

Ty felt as if someone had caught him a short hook under the ribs. The varsity should have smeared the second team all over the field. And they hadn't. They'd looked bad.

He realized abruptly that a team that has bogged down doesn't just suddenly start clicking. They would need everything they had against Ridgewood, and a lot of what they'd had once and should have kept was gone in lost scrimmages. You couldn't buy those back. You couldn't just snap your fingers and say, "Okay, let's go back to where we were when we were a team."

If they were to have even an outside chance against Ridgewood, they'd have to work their hearts out. If Ty Henderson was to be the star back on a real team once more, he'd have to throw everything he had into seeing that eleven players, pulled apart, came together again.

The line of his jaw hardened. And on the next play, when Chad Evans broke into the secondary, it was Ty's merciless tackle that brought him down.

Chad got to his feet, shaking his head, and said "Holy smoke!" fervently.

Ty said, "There's more where that came from. Drop around any time," and the linesman who should have stopped the play said, "Pleased to meet you, Mr. Henderson," with vast sincerity.

So, when they got the ball into their own hands again and the line still couldn't shake Ty loose, he didn't, as he would have before, make any cracks. He just hung on a little more grimly and fought a little harder.

And, as the scrimmage went on, they picked up. Not much, but even in that practice, it showed, particularly on defense. Offensively, there wasn't any sparkle in the play. No snap or polish.

They needed time. They needed a couple of weeks.

They had three days.

The bleachers on both sides of the field were packed and howling as the Marshall band blared out the school song and the squads ran out on the field.

Ty felt, instantly, the quick responsive emotion that a crowd always gave him, the actual delight of their focused attention. If ever an afternoon was going to be his, this would be it. The moment the fans spotted him, they roared his name in welcome. He was still Marshall's star. If Marshall won, he would be their hero.

And the Marshall varsity, in three days, had got back some of what it had lost. They had a fighting chance now, a "maybe" chance. He'd been a dope, in a way, not to have seen what Chad had had to tell him —that he was so important to the team he could split them apart or pull them together. It was a satisfying feeling to know they were together now, thanks to him, and to hear Kenny say, "Sock it to 'em, Ty. This is our day."

Marshall won the toss and elected to receive. Ridgewood went into punt formation with their captain, Earl Hanson, dropping back.

Ty waited on the ten-yard stripe. The whistle shrilled, and the kick was high and long. He scooped the ball into his hands and exploded into action, riding the tail of his interference to the twenty-yard stripe, then breaking for the sidelines. A gentleman in a red jersey nailed him on the twenty-three.

Marshall's ball, first and ten.

Pete Holmes made it second and five on a plunge over center, then lost two yards on the next play. Marshall came out of the huddle in double wing back formation, and Ty, smashing off tackle, was rewarded by a wild shriek from the Blue stands. First down on the thirty-four. Ty grinned in satisfaction. They were rolling already.

But the referee's hands were on his hips, and he was calling the play back. Tommy Kraft at tackle had been offside. Ty turned on him, and then abruptly he stopped and bit back his anger. He wanted these guys working for him, not against him. He'd seen what happened the other way. Springing a star back took a line that was fighting the opposition, not a line that was fighting Ty Henderson.

He said, instead, "Take it easy, kid," and Tommy gave him a look as grateful as a cocker spaniel.

They moved into punt formation, Ty back. The surging Ridgewood line rushed him, but it was a nice boot and someone in the stands yelled, "Yeaaa, Henderson!"

Ridgewood's Sam Ullway at left half brought it back to the Red twenty-nine, and the Ridgewood team settled down to doing business over its own counter. They came up over the ball fast. The pass went to Hanson, and Marshall's ends covered for a wide run. Hanson faded, his guards coming back to protect. Marshall flankers saw the danger too late, and the rangy Red captain heaved a long bullet pass.

The right end caught it on his own forty-five, as if he was out chasing butterflies. A first down for Ridgewood, too close to midfield for comfort. The quarterback had imagination and a lot of nerve.

A line plunge hit the fifty; a spinner was stopped on the Marshall forty-nine. On the next play, the ball went to Sam Ullway again who started for the line on what looked like a repeat, then shoveled the leather to Hanson who headed off over tackle. Choo-Choo blasted through to smash the play, and Ullway lateraled to his fullback who had faked a wide run. The full picked the ball off his shoelaces and shot into open territory.

It was smart tactics and it worked. "Get him. Get that guy," shrieked the Marshall rooters, as the runner ripped his way toward the goal posts. They got him, but he was on the Blue eighteen and Marshall was in real trouble. Kenny called for a time out.

Pete Holmes breathed, "Oh, brother!" Ty scowled. It looked as if they were up against a team with a trunkful of highly coordinated football.

"We'll hold 'em. Dig in, fellows."

They dug so deep they were tunneling, while the Blue stands whipped up a frenzied "Hold that line!" and the Red chanted, "We want a touchdown!"

A smash at center picked up barely three yards when Biff Cassidy refused to be taken out. Second and seven. The Ridgewood quarterback dug into his top hat and pulled out a rabbit in the form of a fake spinner, but Marshall, defensively on edge, was watching for magic and the runner was hit so hard on the eleven that his helmet bounced off, bringing the screaming Blue stands to their feet in the false hope it was the ball. Third and three.

Ridgewood's quarter called on his armored tank for another brutal thrust at center. It wasn't Biff Cassidy's afternoon for giving ground, and when the smoke cleared away it was still three yards to go. Ty glanced at Biff with quick, surprised respect. He hadn't realized before the stubbornness that guy in the middle could show. It was coming in very handy.

Ridgewood went into a huddle to think it out, while the stands held their breaths and the Marshall varsity took long slow ones to relax the building tension.

The Red played it safe and smart. They elected to try for a field goal. Hanson walked back slowly, pulled off his helmet and hiked up his pants. Silence weighted the field as crowd and players hung on the whistle.

Then it came. The ball snapped to the kneeling Ullway who caught and balanced it as Hanson ran forward. Hanson's foot connected with a solid thud as the Marshall line plunged through. The ball soared over their heads, turning lazily against the sky, split the crossbar and fell into the end zone.

Ridgewood, 3; Marshall, 0.

Hanson kicked off. Ty, his fingers itching for the ball, picked it up on his own seventeen, got to the twenty-eight behind fair interference, argued it out for three more yards and hit the dirt on the thirty-one.

Kenny in the huddle gave the nod to Pete, and the fullback lugged the pigskin between right guard and center, picking up four yards. Kenny gave it to him again, and Ty shot a swift look at the quarterback. He wanted to tote the ball himself for some real yardage.

Pete, running so low he practically cut a furrow in the turf with his nose, slugged out two yards; then Kenny swept the end for a first down on the Ridgewood forty-three. The Marshall stands howled their happy surprise, and a lone clarinet in the band echoed it with a sudden hoot.

Well, so long as they were rolling. They could get in scoring position and then shake their star loose.

Steve Hudson at left end said something to Kenny as they lined up, and Kenny nodded.

Signals. "Eighteen—twenty—thirty-one—hep!"

Ty reacted automatically. To the stands, it looked like Pete again. Ridgewood's right tackle slid to cover it, but Kenny took the ball and flipped it to Ty. There was a hole big enough for a victory parade, and Ty flashed through, running hard with high knee-action.

He almost got away, and the hoarse cheering from the Marshall stands was sweet music to his ears. Two outside men in the Red secondary ganged up on him and he pivoted and whirled away, then straightarmed another threat and battled his way to the Ridgewood twenty on a surprise play that had caught the Ridgewood defense wide open.

The Marshall cheerleader led an organized cheer for Ty Henderson, as Ridgewood called for time out. Pete Holmes said, "Nice running, Ty."

Ty nodded, accepting the praise as his due. They hadn't seen anything yet. If they'd just get him loose, he'd make it a field day for Marshall.

Kenny said, "We owe that one to Steve. He tipped me off that the Ridgewood tackle was sliding behind the line of scrimmage. Every time the guy figured he could guess the play, he rolled with it and left his territory wide open." He grinned. "Thanks to Steve, we cashed in."

The "thanks to Steve" business took the edge off Ty's run. He scowled. A whale of a lot of use Steve's brainwave would have been without the ball carrier. It was thanks to Ty that they were deep in enemy territory with a chance to score.

Then he shrugged. It was his name the cheerleader was feeding to the crowd, so why get excited?

He glanced toward the sidelines. Kind of rough on Chad, he thought, being stuck on the bench in the big game. It was sudden warmth for Chad that turned him toward Steve and made him say, "That was real headwork, kid. Nice going."

Steve and Kenny both looked pleased. The warm feeling inside Ty spread.

The time out ended, and Marshall came up on the line fast with the Blue fans yelling. Kenny signaled a pass. Ty faded and hurled a long one downfield. It skidded off the end's grasping fingertips, and the moan from the Marshall gallery was like a storm coming up. Second and ten.

Marshall went into a huddle. "Remember that number eight play?" Kenny said. They remembered it. Razzle-dazzle, and made to order. The ball went to Pete who bucked and flat-passed to Kenny. Kenny stepped back and lateraled to Ty, who spun and whipped a bullet heave downfield to the waiting end.

Calamity was riding the ball. The timing was faulty and Ridgewood intercepted, as the Ridgewood stands surged to their feet.

Ty jerked his helmet off and slammed it down on the ground. It was a clockwork play, and the clock had run slow. It wasn't any use kidding. The play had shown up Marshall's offensive fault, lack of coordination. You could lay it to only one thing, the practice scrimmages of a team that hadn't been working together. They should have had that play under their belts if it was to click in a big game. And they hadn't.

Marshall's big scoring chance in the first half was gone, because until only a few days ago the varsity had been travelling eleven ways at once. And it was Ridgewood's ball again.

Right away, they brought it back up over the midfield stripe. When the gun ended the second half, it was a welcome sound.

Ty walked off the field slowly, hope draining out of him. Marshall wasn't going to win. The stuff that Ty Henderson had to deliver wasn't going to get a chance to show. There'd been too much lost in those practices. It was too-little-and-too-late now.

The locker room was quiet and businesslike. Chad dropped down on a bench beside Ty. Ty said, "How's it look?"

Chad shook his head. "I don't know. Ridgewood's got quite a team."

Emphasis on the team. Ty's fists curled up. "If they could only get me loose—"

"You still thinking about that, Ty?"

Ty knew what Chad meant. He said defensively, "I did all right, didn't I, with that run?"

"Steve saw the tackle being sucked in."

So Chad had noticed that too. Ty said "Yeah" and

sat staring at the floor. This was his day, and it was going haywire. Worse than that, Chad thought that Ty was to blame. Because he'd started working with the team too late, so that now when they needed all the edge and nerve and drive and coordination they could get, they didn't have it. And Ridgewood did.

Marshall kicked off to open the second half, and right away they were in trouble. Hanson flashed to midfield behind solid interference, and two short passes gave the Red a first down on Marshall's thirty-eight. Marshall gave ground with the Blue rooters pleading frantically.

Forced into the shadow of their own goal posts, they fought back desperately, but the Ridgewood powerhouse was really rolling and the tempo of the play was brutal. Ty, backing up the defense, had a feeling he'd never had before except when he was running the ball. A feeling of scrapping for every inch of green turf. Somehow, some way, Ridgewood had to be stopped.

He batted down a pass and the stands roared. He smashed into a tackle and nobody noticed. He kept on smashing doggedly, because all he cared about was that outside chance. All he wanted was the leather in his own hands again. All right, so his teammates couldn't shake him loose. He'd shake himself loose. Just get the ball away from this driving, merciless machine.

Marshall got a break. The referee called a holding penalty on Ridgewood, and the fifteen-yard loss stopped them momentarily. With only two downs to make the distance, Ridgewood tried a pass. Incomplete. Then Hugh Lawrence broke up an end sneak and Marshall took the ball on downs.

It was a tight corner for the kicker, and Ty felt a hollow inside him. If the line didn't hold—

The line held. Marshall might not have any scoring punch, but defensively the Blue was in there slugging. He was fast getting the punt away, and he kept it out of the receiver's eager hands. The Marshall stands drew a deep breath of impassioned relief.

And Ridgewood started on another big push.

The third quarter, for Marshall, was a weary stubborn battle all the way. They got shoved back and back, with the play concentrated between the Blue goal line and midfield. For Marshall, it was all defensive and they relied heavily on Ty's punting. It was sober satisfaction to him that he could do that job, but it was a long way from what he wanted and he raged inwardly against the fate that kept him bottled up.

The final quarter slid into the same despairing groove.

Ty knew they had lost the game. The guys playing alongside him knew it. They couldn't pierce that armor plate, and it was almost a miracle that they had managed to keep Ridgewood from another score, after that one goal from the field. The only possible chance for Marshall now would be a field-long play, a break play from deep in their own territory.

Ty pictured it yearningly—himself lugging the ball, head down, feet flying. Over the midfield stripe, into the open, blazing and fighting and ripping his way to the score that would win the game.

He came down to earth with a jolt. It was Ridge-wood's ball, and time was running out.

Ty felt sudden hopeless anger. He'd wanted his team to win. He'd wanted to carry the mail on a dazzling run. And, instead, the whole afternoon had been spent absorbing a murderous pounding. They'd held. Oh, sure, they'd held. They'd hung on until they were so tired now that when they came up on the line they were slow. They were so tired they'd give yard by yard, until Ridgewood was camped in dangerous territory again. And then they'd stiffen.

He was doing it himself. He didn't know why. There wasn't much sense in this endless diving in, being knocked down, getting up again, being knocked down again. He ached all over. Let Ridgewood carry the ball across, he thought savagely. What difference did it make? The score might as well be ten to nothing, as three to nothing.

Chad had been right. The time had been too short to rebuild a team. Maybe after this game, this blasted game that meant so much to Marshall—

There was a sudden, deep-throated roar from the Marshall stands. The Ridgewood center made a fuzzy pass, and the Red full chased it back ten yards. Marshall caught him there, and Ridgewood had twelve yards to make on fourth down. The ball was near the sidelines, no place for another field goal and no down to waste running it out.

There was time for maybe two more plays. Ridge-wood, leisurely in the huddle, killed a sneak into the line, and Marshall took the ball on downs.

The timekeeper had his gun out. In the stands, there

was a surge of movement as the crowd edged forward, waiting for the end of play, Marshall hopeless, Ridgewood triumphant.

Marshall's ball on their own eighteen.

Kenny said, "We'll shoot a pass." They all nodded. One last desperate gamble, and then it would be over and done with. Ty, looking at them, had a quick sense of pride. They were so tired, and they'd fought so hard, and they were still willing to shoot passes.

They came out of the huddle. Biff at center fed the ball to Ty. Ty faded.

It was obvious that a pass was Marshall's only chance. The end was already streaking downfield. Ridgewood covered.

And the Ridgewood tackle, overconfident again, slid ahead of the play.

Ty saw the hole out of the corner of his eye. It was just about wide enough for a scared mouse to wiggle through, but maybe— Just maybe.

Ty suddenly tucked the ball he had been about to throw under one arm and headed for that piece of daylight. The sudden change in plans threw the whole field wide open and shattered the offensive assignments. His gang would have to figure it out for themselves.

He streaked for his chink of daylight and plunged through it, running so hard that, when no one stopped him where he expected to be stopped, he overran himself and almost fell. Someone was picking up on interference fast. There wasn't time to stop and ask names.

The midfield stripe sprang up ahead of him. The Marshall rooters were jumping and yelling and waving books, flags, hats. Ty, his feet and heart pounding, crossed the fifty, saw a Ridgewood tackle looming up, checked, whirled and reversed his field.

Half the Ridgewood team was on the tail of those flying cleats, and it was pandemonium in the bleachers. Ty raced down the sidelines. Headline hopes that he had given up raced with him. Ty Henderson Hero in Last-Second Marshall Win. Brilliant Run by Star Half—

He could win this race. He knew he could. He was leading the field, and not a man on the Ridgewood team was fast enough to touch him.

And then he saw that, ahead of him, at the end of the touchdown stretch, was Ridgewood's Eric Hanson. Too smart a safety to be pulled out when the play exploded, he was braced to meet the runner near the angle of the end zone, where sideline stripes and goal line met.

Ty added it up fast. He could run over Hanson, bowl him out of the way. He had to, and he could. He shifted the ball, ready for a straightarm.

And, as he shifted, he saw that Kenny Simons was racing parallel with him. It was anybody's guess how Kenny had gotten there, but there he was, high, wide and anxious. And waiting.

Waiting for a lateral, with a clear field ahead of him for a touchdown.

Instinctively, Ty's fingers tightened around the ball, pulling it in against him defiantly. This was Ty Henderson's play.

The Ridgewood safety couldn't stop him. He would go over him, through him. Under him, if he had to.

But nobody else was going to carry that ball to glory and gone, except a halfback named Henderson. This was what he'd been working for. This was why he'd strung along with Chad, cooperated with the team, fought side by side with them all afternoon. This was football, Ty Henderson's kind of football.

Ty Henderson's kind of football.

It was like a slap across his face. Ty Henderson, who had been teamed up all afternoon with a bunch of guys who had played their hearts out. Guys who had been slugging it out, shoulder to shoulder, with him.

He remembered the warm feeling he'd had digging in with them on defense. The sense of helplessness when a play hadn't clicked. The pride in a team that stuck till the final gun.

And, above all, the pride in a fellow like Chad who had played his ball game on the bench so that his team would have a chance.

Hanson was crouched to spring. The split Ridgewood defense was hot on Ty's heels. This was it. Glory for him? Or glory for Kenny?

Glory for Marshall.

He flipped the ball, light as a feather and accurate as a compass, straight into Kenny's hands. Then he threw a block that wiped Eric Hanson clean off the slate.

Kenny crossed the line standing up, and the packed dynamite of the Marshall stands exploded with a deafening roar.

Ty got to his feet a little dizzily. Marshall, 6; Ridgewood, 3.

He looked down at Hanson, and reached out a helping hand. The score was inescapable, and he didn't want to rub it in, but just the same he needed words to express the swell feeling inside himself.

"Well," said Ty Henderson, "how do you like our team?"

TOO CLOSE TO NATURE

TIP TAYLOR reared up out of the Sunday paper and waved a section of it triumphantly. "Here it is," he announced happily, spreading the piece out on the floor and spreading himself over it.

Doug Brown joined him, full length. "Essay contest," he read obediently. "Sponsored by the Middletown Outdoors Association. Get your elbow off the page, pal. Hmmm. One hundred prizes offered for the best essays submitted on any aspect of outdoor life. Hmmm, again. Thrice hmmm."

"They had practically the same thing last year," said Tip, heaving up and down in an enthralled manner and endangering Doug's literary life. "Bugs Harrison won that movie camera."

"I remember." He gazed at Tip dreamily. "We could use a movie camera. Or a tennis racket or two. Or a printing outfit. You can't lose anyway, with a hundred chances at a prize. The last fifty prizes are books. Can you read?"

"No," said Tip, "but I have a friend named Douglas who's halfway through the alphabet."

"Bright fellow," Doug approved, then rolled over on his back and gazed judicially at the ceiling. "Now, the question is, what shall we write about? We need a good fruity subject."

"Swimming?"

"That's damp, not fruity. How about tennis?"

Tip shook his head. "We want something more colorful. Skiing would be all right, but this is sort of an off-season."

Doug agreed that July was indeed an off-season for skiing. He said it probably had something to do with the lack of snow, which in turn was influenced by the warm weather. He then told Tip not to be a dope and returned to studying the ceiling.

There was a short silence. Then,

"Deep sea fishing?" said Tip hopefully.

"Ideal," said Doug, withering the suggestion. "You bring the deep sea, and I'll bring the fish."

"Mountain climbing?"

"I suppose you have a mountain in your pocket?"

"Certainly," said Tip. "Just take a peak." He rolled over out of reach of Doug's foot and remarked sadly that no one appreciated him.

"*I* appreciate you, Mr. Bones," Doug said, "but you can sit down now and can the wisecracks."

Tip clasped his hands and cooed happily. "My pal! Do you really think they're good enough to be preserved?" This time, he dodged too late and got Doug's shoe in his ribs which took him temporarily out of the conversation, a difficult thing to do with Tip.

However, the unwonted silence had a stimulating effect on Doug's brain, and he leaped suddenly to his
feet. "I've got it! Camping!"

"Camping?"

"Certainly. What does the Outdoors Association
specialize in? Nature. And what could possibly bring
you closer to Nature than camping?"

Tip looked uncertain. "But isn't camping rather
difficult? I mean, don't you have to have equipment,
and know how to make a fire with two sticks and all
that kind of thing?"

"Nonsense," said Doug briskly. "You're thinking of
the Boy Scouts. *Anybody* can go out in the woods and
camp." He struck a pose. "I can see it all now. The sun
sinking in the west, the stars twinkling overhead, the
first pink glow of dawn. . . ."

"All at the same time?" said Tip, worried.

"Of course not. Stop cramping my style. Look, Tip,
all we have to do is throw a few things together in a
duffel-bag. It's simple."

"Oh," said Tip. "What's a duffel-bag?"

"How should I know? I suppose it's a thing they
keep duffels in." Doug waved the question aside.
"We'll write as we go along, and the thing will be tremendous."

"Colossal," said Tip, "I hope."

"Superb. We've as good as won a movie camera already. Come, my boy, we have work to do."

Tip came.

The next afternoon, they barged forth happily on
their back-to-Nature movement, lightly equipped
with what Doug insisted on calling the "basic necessi-

ties." He felt this was a good phrase for their essay, and the only articles in which he took a really deep interest were notebook, pencil and food.

"Shouldn't we borrow a compass?" said Tip, affected by a vague notion that a compass was highly woodsmanlike.

"Of course not," said Doug scornfully. "There you go again, making noises like a Boy Scout. We'll travel by the sun. After all, we're supposed to be tossing away the trappings of civilization. Make a note of that, Tip. It sounds significant."

Tip hauled forth their notebook and made a note of it. "Do you spell civilization with an s or z?" he inquired. Doug said it didn't matter, as they were leaving it behind. He then took a deep breath and said "Hark!"

Tip said, "Huh?"

"Hark," said Doug again, frowning slightly. "A nature lover always harks. In this case, we are harking to the cheery twitter of our little friends, the birds."

"Those are Mr. Bailey's chickens."

"Oh." Doug rallied rapidly. "Well, never mind. Put our feathered friends in anyhow, and we'll add more notes later. We now head west to the woods. Good. I rather fancy myself journeying into the setting sun."

"Leaving the setting hens behind us in the east. It seems a sound idea."

"Make a memorandum, but leave the hens out. They strike the wrong note." Doug inhaled deeply three or four times and started out briskly, in long strides. Tip, whose legs were shorter, galloped beside him, licking the point of his pencil alertly. Doug began to dictate. "Overhead," he intoned, "a brilliant sun beams from a cloudless sky. Well, not quite cloudless maybe, but why be technical?"

"The paper said rain," Tip offered.

Doug frowned upwards. "Nonsense. Just a few stout clouds, hanging rather low. It's a beautiful day."

"Okay," said Tip, making notes. "Brilliant sun, cloudless sky— Got it. I think I hear a bird. Do you want to get him in?"

"It's just a crow—they don't count. Did you ever hear of anyone harking to a crow? Put your notebook away for a while, my boy. We're still too close to town. Slowly, slowly, the petty cares of the world drop away, as we leave the busy, everyday world behind us. Muted is the hum of the factory, silenced the mighty— What's that fancy word that means a lot of noise?"

"Din?"

"Din, nothing! Where's your soul? Cacophony's the word I want."

"You can have it."

"—silenced the mighty cacophony of modern living. I hope you're getting all this down."

"You," said Tip, aggrieved, "told me to put the notebook away."

"Did I now? Well, get it out again. The gentle, lulling voice of Nature speaks from every tree. Or it would if that crow would shut up. The—"

"I can't spell it."

"You can't spell what?"

"Ca-whatsit. The thing that makes a noise."

"Of all the dopes! C-a-c-a-p—no, c-a-c-o-p. Just put Cac. I'll know what you mean."

"More'n I do," Tip complained, writing busily. "What was that bit about Nature speaking?"

"That's where we harked. The gentle, lulling voice of Nature speaks from every tree. The little furred denizens of the woods peer out from the underbrush, wishing the travelers well. Put your shoulders back, Tippy."

"Back where?"

"Just back. Breathe Nature's pure ozone. Be an outdoor man like me." Doug hit himself on the chest and gave a hollow cough. "And take longer strides, my boy. We've got to be at a camping site by nightfall."

"It's all very well for you," said Tip, his pencil joggling. "You don't have to take dictation while you walk."

"In that case, ship your pencil and just walk. I'll turn on the literature again when we're huddled over our glowing campfire."

"Isn't it kind of hot to huddle?"

Doug looked at him pleadingly. "We *have* to have a campfire, Tip. Apart from cooking, who ever heard of a camp without a campfire? Do you or do you not want a motion picture camera?"

"I do. Always bearing in mind that we might get a printing press."

"In that case, we'll print our essay and distribute it around the neighborhood. Tip, this is really a splendid idea even if there weren't a contest. I feel like a new man."

At this moment, Tip gave a squawk of anguish, having wedded himself firmly to a blackberry bush that refused to get out of his way. Doug, extricating him, was perfectly cheerful. "We can put that in the essay, slightly fictionized," he said brightly. "Something about how Nature draws us closer to her as we venture into the wilderness."

"Wilderness is just the word I've been groping for," said Tip bitterly. "I think we're off the trail."

"We can't be. The sun's right in front." He looked around wildly. "Where *is* the sun?"

"In the west."

"Where's the west?"

"Right behind the sun. I see what you mean, though. They've been and put clouds all over the place." Tip stared around him. "What do you do when there's no sun to tell directions by? I told you we should bring a compass."

"You look for moss on a tree or something," Doug said vaguely.

"Isn't there some trick way of telling north by looking at your watch?"

"Impossible," Doug said decidedly. "You do get the wildest ideas."

"I read about it somewhere." Tip shrugged. "Oh, well, what's the difference? We're in the woods, which is all that matters, and we can settle in any likely camping spot." At that convenient instant, they stepped into a clearing which was about the size of a table top. "Ha," said Tip, and sat down.

"Hey," said Doug, "we can't stay here. It's too early to strike camp."

"To what?"

"Strike camp."

Tip said he had never struck an innocent little camp in his life and wasn't going to start now. He said the camp had done him no harm. He further said that his feet hurt and he wanted to stay right where he was.

"No," said Doug gallantly. "We are pressing on."

"I left my flatiron home. All right, all right. Forward, press."

They started off again, walking doggedly. They walked. They walked some more. They continued to walk, and the woods grew deeper. Tip began to mutter. "Courage," said Doug. "I see a clearing ahead."

Tip picked up speed, and they both bounded forth once more into an open space. It was a small open space, about the size of a table top. It had a rather familiar look.

"It's true then," said Tip softly.

Doug sounded cross. "What's true?"

"The world is round. We've walked twenty-five thousand miles, and we're back where we started. How about a line or two regarding the immutable laws of Nature?"

"Oh, shuddup," said Doug. "These woods are following us around."

"We're lost," said Tip.

"Nonsense. At the worst, we're slightly mislaid."

"You're mislaid. I'm lost. And I think it's going to rain."

Doug glanced at the sky. "Clear as crystal, except for the clouds. You know, Tip, you're being very tiresome. This whole thing was your idea."

"It was *not* my idea. I was browsing innocently through a newspaper, and— You know what? I'm hungry." Having thus diagnosed the cause of his general ill-will, Tip immediately cheered up and began poking through his sack for nourishment.

"Okay, we'll eat. But first we need a fire. Where's the notebook?"

Tip wailed. "You can't start a fire with the notebook, after all that dictation I took so patiently. It ain't ethical."

"I don't want to start a fire with it. I want to dictate some more." Doug cleared his throat executively. "The campers, pleasantly weary, turn gaily to the problem of fuel."

"Gaily?" said Tip.

"Certainly. Building a fire is very simple. People just tell you it's hard so you'll think they're clever. Nothing to it at all." He gazed around him thoughtfully. "Here, Tippy, give me the notebook, and I'll write while you get sticks."

"Division of labor, bah," said Tip, but departed. When he came back, Doug had a dreamy look of creative frenzy and was no help at all. Tip, grumbling, began to pile the wood up in a hopeful position and hauled forth matches. He struck one carefully and applied it to his edifice. The match went out. Tip struck another. That went out. He struck a third.

Doug, who had been rhapsodizing about eager flames, glanced up. The third match gave a sputter and followed its brothers into extinguishment. Tip said, "There must be more to building a fire than you thought."

"Here. Try this." Doug ripped out a piece of paper and handed it over. "It says in my notes that the eager flames curl upward, and in a moment the delicious nostalgic scent of wood-smoke fills the air."

Tip tried the paper and produced the last half of the sentence. He then said hopefully that where there was smoke there was fire. He then looked for the fire. It was not there. "Then, where," said Tip, coughing slightly, "is the smoke coming from? It's most unreasonable."

Doug crawled over to investigate and offer more paper. Just as this got nicely ignited, he discovered that he had flung away his observations on fire-building. However the writing appeared to be realistic enough to have some effect, and a small flame decided to stay. Tip blew on it tenderly and gave a satisfied squawk. "Don't know how long it'll last, though. We'd better work fast."

Doug leaped for the pancake mix and Tip's canteen of water, dumping both into their saucepan and stirring them around devotedly. Tip planked the frying pan down on the fire, unwrapped some limp pieces of bacon and threw them in. The longest piece curled up like a caterpillar, but the other victims responded to first-aid treatment, and the delicious scents which Doug had been babbling about began to fill the air.

Tip draped the finished bacon over his canteen, there being no other bacon-draping equipment handy, and laid it tenderly on the ground beside him, while Doug, with a flourish, poured the pancake batter into the frying pan. The flapjack began to turn golden-brown, and Tip gave a luxurious sniff of anticipation. Doug drew a deep breath. "The rich scents of cooking mingle with the night air," he orated, "as the fire crackles and blazes. The flapjacks, golden-brown and feather-light, come forth tempting and piping-hot from the skillet. —Tip, how the dickens do I turn this thing over?"

"You give the pan a flip and the flapjack flops."

"Oh." Doug grasped the handle firmly, shrieked and began to dance around in a weird ritual. Tip watched him for a moment with grave interest, then got the idea and efficiently wound his handkerchief around the hot handle. Doug, growling, seized it again, took another deep breath and gave a heave. The pan flipped. The flapjack flopped.

Unfortunately, it flopped into the fire. Tip put his head in his hands. There was a short but eloquent silence. "Missed it," said Doug, after a moment.

"You did, indeed," said Tip.

Doug braced his shoulders. "Well, well. Never say die. There's plenty more batter. Pass me the saucepan."

Tip passed it. "The bacon's getting cold," he murmured and glanced over his shoulder at the object of his worries. He then gave a howl of wrath. The canteen was undraped; the bacon was gone. From a far-off branch, a squirrel complained bitterly about its digestion. "You and your furry friends!" said Tip. "That beastly animal snitched our dinner. I hope he gets hiccoughs."

Doug poured batter and tried to be impartial. "After all, we're supposed to be getting close to Nature. Cheer up, Tippy. We can cook some more bacon."

They crouched side by side over the fire and watched

their new flapjack with devoted interest. Once more
a beautiful golden-brown rewarded them. "Now!" said
Doug between his teeth. He seized the handle and
tossed. The flapjack went up, the flapjack came down.
Miraculously, it came down in the pan. Tip led a cheer
and hauled out two tin plates. In a few minutes, the
beautiful round object was declared done. "To a turn,"
said Doug, "whatever that means."

He scooped it out of the pan and laid it reverently on
Tip's plate. Tip seized a tin fork and hacked it down
the center, depositing half on Doug's. Doug dropped
three more pieces of bacon into the frying pan, ignored
them firmly and raised his own fork in salute to a
splendid meal.

Tip took a large bite. Doug followed suit. They began
to chew. They continued to chew. After a moment, Tip
looked down at his shoes, but they were still on his feet.
It had occurred to him that, in some manner, they
might have crept into the frying pan and substituted
themselves for Doug's flapjacks. Whatever the flapjacks were made of, then, it was not shoe leather. It
was a consoling thought.

"Doug," said Tip softly, still chewing.

Doug nodded. He, too, had had an instant's wonder
about the shoes. He had also had an alternative theory
that they might be eating one of the duffel-bags, nicely
fried, but both duffel-bags were still in evidence.

"Strange," said Doug.

"Resilient, aren't they?" said Tip, chewing gamely.

"It may be," Doug suggested, "that we're sitting
under a rubber tree."

"Make a wonderful automobile tire." Ted picked up

the box of pancake flour and stared at it fixedly for a moment, then gave a yelp.

" 'Smatter?"

An outraged splutter answered him. "It's plain flour, you silly coot," said Tip indignantly. "You packed the wrong box. We're sitting here trying to eat fried flour and water. You—you *woodsman,* you!"

At this moment, Doug leaped to his feet and rescued the bacon. It was certainly crisp, but it was also entirely black.

In the end, they dined frugally on apples, cookies and a handful of dried figs. Darkness found them hunched dejectedly over a few embers and a saucepanful of flour and water paste.

"Well," said Doug, getting slowly to his feet, "I suppose we might as well turn in. Unroll your blanket, pardner." He took a hefty swat at the air and scowled. "If that's a mosquito—"

"What's it look like?"

"A DC-4 with a beak."

"It's a mosquito then." Tip took a couple of swats himself, scored near misses and borrowed Doug's scowl. "You pack any citronella?"

"Any what?"

"Citronella."

"If that's the lady with the glass slipper," said Doug, "no."

Tip raised his eyes to heaven and prayed for strength. "Citronella is mosquito dope, dope."

"Oh. In that case, nope, dope, I didn't. Pull your blanket over your head." He spread his own out carefully on the ground, lay on one end and rolled himself into a careful cocoon. "In the healing arms of sleep," said Doug, "under Nature's vast skies— Tip, put the fire out, will you?"

"*And* the cat?" said Tip bitterly. "And wind the clock?"

"Un'h." Doug, his nose just peering over the blanket, seemed to be in a difficult mood. This was not altogether unreasonable, as he had wound himself up so tightly that his arms were helpless, and a mosquito was sitting on his nose, sighting down its proboscis. There was a sudden upheaval, and Doug, blanket and visitor all rose in the air. Score one for Nature.

Tip kicked the fire apart—it consisted of one ember —and returned to his own downy rest. He inserted himself into his blanket with a grateful sigh and relaxed with a long-drawn-out "Ahhhh." For two minutes exactly, he lay still, then he reared up and took a punch at what would have been his pillow if he had had a pillow. The unyielding ground punched him back. Tip gave a furious howl and clutched his damaged paw.

Doug said wearily, "*Now* what's the matter?"

"The soft lap of Nature," said Tip sardonically. "It's full of rocks."

"If you think *you've* got trouble," Doug invited, "come on over here. It's my opinion we took the wrong route, and this is the Rock of Gibraltar. I always thought you were supposed to lie under the vast dome of night, watching the stars in the velvet sky as you slipped off into gentle dreamless slumber."

Tip said blackly, "There must be some way of arranging a bed outdoors so you don't feel as if a whole family of porcupines had crawled in with you. Ouch!" He sat up to conduct a survey, was faintly relieved to find they were only twigs, and lay down again. The mosquitoes, who had been bustling around with their sleeves rolled up to develop an appetite, now got down to business in earnest, and in a moment Doug's and Tip's blankets were humped-up and outraged battlegrounds.

After a while, Doug's dim, defeated voice arose. "*I am going under my blanket*," he said hopelessly. "Call me if the phone rings."

Tip promised he would. He then added thoughtfully, "Of course, you'll smother. But what's that to me?" He then went under his own blanket. After a long time, the mosquitoes, irked, drifted away. Doug reappeared, chanting imprecations against the stone quarry he was lying on. "What time is it, Tip?"

"Can't see my watch," said Tip. "It's got its hands in front of its face." He then added, more factually, "Its pitch dark, you lunatic."

"Strike a match."

"I will not. All the mosquitoes will come back. Doug—"

"What?"

"Nothing. I was just thinking about my bed at home. It's got pillows on it, you know. Real pillows." He sighed. "Don't people make beds out of pine boughs or something?"

Doug grunted. "No. They'd be full of needles. And don't tell me you read it in any books, and, anyway, shut up. You're pillowed in Nature's gracious arms, in case you don't know it, and you're being lulled to sleep—"

up very clearly. The only mystery was how they had managed to lose it. It led them forth. In fact, it offered the final insult; it led straight to civilization in less than five minutes, and with civilization the bitter discovery that they could have spent the night in a nice, dry barn.

They were both rather thoughtful on the journey home. Speaking between sneezes, Tip inquired what they were going to do about the essay. Replying between sneezes of his own, Doug said savagely that they would just go ahead and write the beastly thing.

They wrote their essay the following afternoon, when their sneezes were more subdued and they had a dictionary handy to describe the unutterable raptures of outdoor life. The way they put it, camping sounded rather fine, and Tip re-read the finished product with a puzzled frown. "Very appealing," he observed. "I don't understand it."

"Go on and mail it," said Doug sternly. "And get out of my sight."

It was ten days before they heard from the Middletown Outdoors Association, and then a package arrived. It was rather a small package, and Doug dashed over to Tip's house with it at once, making sounds of victory. "It isn't a movie camera," he conceded, poking the wrappings, "but still it's a prize. I think it's a book."

"Maybe," said Tip, pawing the paper off.

It was a book. They took it out and looked at it. It was a small book with a paper cover. At the top of the cover it said "Handbook for Boys." At the bottom, it said "Boy Scouts of America."

Tip turned it around and around in his hands, gazing

at it thoughtfully. "Oh," he said. Then he looked at Doug rather uncomfortably. "Uh, Doug, maybe *you'd* better keep this."

"Uh—no, thank you," said Doug politely. "You keep it."

"Well, I—er—I don't *need* it exactly," said Tip.

"I don't need it either."

"It looks—very interesting," said Tip.

"*You* keep it."

Tip rubbed his nose unhappily. "Well, I—well, as a matter of fact, Doug— As a matter of fact—" He drew a deep breath and went on hurriedly. "As a matter of fact, Doug, I *have* a copy already."

Doug looked at him. "You *have* a copy?"

Tip looked vaguely guilty. "Yes, I got to thinking, and well— Well, to tell you the truth, Doug, I've been and went and joined the Boy Scouts. I know you never want to hear about camping again, but—" He pushed the handbook firmly under Doug's nose. "It won't hurt you just to read it, Doug. For instance, about making fires."

Doug took the book, looked at it sternly and then tossed it aside. "No," said Doug.

"No?"

"No." Doug shook his head emphatically. "I know all I want to know about building fires."

"You don't know much," said Tip.

"I know as much as you do." Doug drew himself up with great dignity and looked Tip straight in the eye. "As a matter of fact, my friend," he said, "you are speaking to a fellow Scout. I joined last week."

There was a faint gurgle. That was Tip speaking.

"And don't just stand there and smirk at me," said Doug. "Next year, we'll write a real essay and maybe we'll win a—a—"

"A movie camera?" said Tip.

"A camping outfit," said Doug, settling the matter once and for all.

DOUBLE FAULT

THE shoelace snapped.

Any self-respecting shoelace would have snapped after the violent tug Rocky Turner had given it, but Rocky's point of view was that the shoelace manufacturer had made his product out of spider webs and wet blotting paper. Why, he demanded hotly, couldn't they ever get decent shoelaces around there?

Jim Ellis, parked on a locker bench and fiddling with his tennis racket, sighed, reached into his own locker and tossed over a new pair of laces. "Relax, pal."

Rocky gave a half-hearted snort of grievance. "Every time I look at a shoelace lately, it snaps."

"You probably snapped at it first," said Jim. Then he looked thoughtful for a moment and added, "Look, Rocky, be a good egg and try to get through this match without blowing up in the middle of it, will you? The heat's going to be bad enough without—"

"Me?" said Rocky. "What makes you think I'd blow up?"

"Observation," Jim murmured, rather sadly.

79

"Oh, well—" Rocky waved an airy hand. "I just happen to be the temperamental type. Don't you fret, sonny boy."

Jim twirled his racket between his fingers. "The Andrews twins are pretty hot stuff, and this *is* the City title we're playing for. I only meant—"

Rocky patted him kindly on the head. "Don't worry. We'll breeze right through it, so just keep calm. Papa will take care of you and hold your hand."

"Just hold your own hand and keep yourself calm is all I ask," said Jim. "Come on, slowpoke." He retrieved Rocky's eyeshade from under the bench, slung a towel over his shoulder and led the way out of the cool stillness of the locker room to the baking heat of the courts.

Their appearance was greeted by wild cheers from the West High gallery, which Rocky acknowledged with a wave of his racket. Then he joined Jim at the umpire's chair, where the lanky Andrews brothers, defending the title for Jefferson High, were already waiting.

The sun, high and hot in a flat cloudless sky, blazed down on the courts, and the air shimmered and danced in the windless heat. Rocky cocked his eyeshade over one eye and shifted his racket lightly in his hand.

Tod Andrews' serve had wildcats in it, and it came leaping over the net with speed to burn. Rocky's snapback return lit in Dick Andrews' alley, cuddled to the corner, and Dick socked it back deep.

Jim with a beautiful placement shot, forced a short return. Rocky raced in to smash the ball murderously, and it turned up its toes and died on the further side of the net. Someone in the West gallery applauded,

and Rocky sketched a salute with his racket, nodding to Jim.

"Hi, champ. What did I tell you? It's a pushover."

Jim raised an eyebrow and said, "I hope, I hope."

The next serve launched a long violent rally, with the spectators' heads following the ball's flight like so many puppets jerked on strings, and then Dick Andrews' blazing forehand drive took the point for Jefferson.

"Whoosh," said Rocky thoughtfully, having been doing a considerable amount of traveling.

He looked even more thoughtful when the Jefferson pair produced a net and baseline bombardment that clicked off three points in succession. "Game," said the umpire, and someone in the front row of the Jefferson gallery crowed with approval.

Rocky scowled at the sun, then shrugged and walked back confidently to the baseline. He had a mean and powerful cannonball serve, and he put everything he had into the first one, just to destroy any fond illusions that the Andrews twins might be cherishing.

The ball winged over the net and exploded in Tod's court, but Tod, instead of folding up politely with shock, cut it back with plenty of snap. Rocky shoveled, and Dick responded with a screaming drive down the center of the court. Jim lobbed, gaining time. Tod volleyed from mid-court, and Jim burned it back at an impossible angle, and deep.

The point was so obviously lost that the umpire had his mouth open to "Fifteen-love" when Tod's racket connected somehow in a desperate, over-the-shoulder shot, and the ball tumbled over the net strap and plopped into Rocky's court.

"Love-fifteen," said the umpire, changing his mind.

Jim, passing Rocky in the back court, said, "Any resemblance between these guys and a pushover is strictly coincidental," and Rocky gave him a quick look, having made that unwelcome discovery for himself. He had thought he knew about what to expect of the Andrews team, figuring that he and Jim could clinch the match in two sets. Now, suddenly, it didn't look so easy. There was this little matter of the way Tod and Dick were playing.

And the way they handled his service and came back for more. He didn't like that. He had never produced more perfectly timed, on-the-ball smashes, but they were being socked right back at him.

He began to feel the heat. The sun was like an oven, and the glare striking up from the court hurt his eyes. He tugged his eyeshade lower, then shoved it back impatiently. The thermometer must be pushing ninety in the sun, and it was all sun out on the baked clay surface.

"Ready?" said the umpire, motioning him to serve.

All through that first set, play seesawed unendurably and every earned point was a major battlefield. "Deuce" became a theme song, and the umpire's voice got monotonous. Then Rocky put them in the lead triumphantly with a reckless, ground-hugging drive that torpedoed crosscourt and exploded in the alley, out of reach of Tod's frantic lunge.

The umpire said "Set point" placidly.

It was Jim's serve and he went back to the baseline, mopping his brow, and stood still for a moment. Then he coiled like a steel spring in his intricate service and scorched the ball over the net. The powerful kick of the serve caught Tod unprepared, and his return was limp. Jim's overhead smash kicked up a faint puff of chalk on the line, and the ball rolled in the alley.

"Game and set to Turner and Ellis," said the umpire.

Rocky joined Jim at the sidelines and caught up a towel. "Confound this heat," he said irritably. "It's like a furnace. What a day for a championship match!"

Jim nodded. "Wish I was made of asbestos. I think those Andrews guys are. Did somebody say 'push-over'?"

"All right, all right. So I was wrong." Rocky's voice got an edge on it.

Jim said equably, "Oh, well. The bigger they are the higher they bounce. An old Russian proverb, or something. Come on, pal, let's finish things up this set."

Rocky went back to position, muttering to himself. Wherever he went the sun seemed to follow, stabbing needles of heat into him, and right away the Jefferson pair opened the set by taking the first two games, picking their points off their shoelaces and out of the sky. The Jefferson gallery was getting pretty worked up, and Rocky began to notice the noise and resent it.

The third game went to deuce and stuck there like a fly in a jampot. "Vantage in—vantage out—vantage in," till Rocky felt his teeth on edge and his grip tightening on the taped handle of his racket.

With the advantage to them, he nearly finished the game with a chop shot, but it dropped just outside the alley and a groan from the West galleries dropped with it. Rocky jerked off his eyeshade and shied it across the court in a gust of nervous exasperation. Why couldn't that have been in? It was too beastly hot—

It was an uphill fight just to keep the score even, the way those Andrews twins kept whacking the ball back. The court felt like the Sahara desert—miles of sun and heat—and it seemed to Rocky the ball was always popping up under his nose again, no matter what he did. He could knock the hide off the thing, smashing it, and still those Andrews brothers sent it right back.

Games 2-all, 3-all, 4-3, in favor of the Jefferson pair. Rocky ran himself into the ground, chasing shots, and somehow they made it 4-all. Then, climaxing a really brilliant rally, 5-4 for Rocky and Jim.

If they got the next game, it was their match. City champions.

A lot of the sting was worn out of Rocky's serve, and Dick Andrews spun back a shot that was tough to handle. Jim, trying too hard, sliced it into the net.

"What in blazes do you think you're doing?" Rocky snapped. "Playing tiddley-winks?"

Jim said, "Sorry."

You could yell at Jim for weeks and all he'd ever say was "Sorry." You might as well fight a sofa pillow. Rocky glared at him in exasperation and stalked back to the baseline. Even his own serve was beginning to act as ornery as a porcupine, and his nerves tightened and crawled as he and Jim fought for a lead.

But "Five games all," said the umpire finally. "Deuce on the set."

"Oh, blast it!" Rocky exploded. He felt as if the sun

had pinned him down permanently to the court, and the racket in his hand weighed a ton.

"We'll still get 'em," Jim promised.

"Oh, *can* the Pollyanna stuff!"

A teaser shot from Tod Andrews' racket stumbled into the net. Love-15. Jim socked a blistering drive to Dick's backhand and scored a clean pass. Love-30. They took that game but lost the next one and bogged down interminably at 6-all before they forced the Andrews boys to the net, lobbed shrewdly over their heads, and jacked the score up to 7-6.

Over and back, over and back the ball went, like the swinging pendulum of a clock.

15-all.

30-15. The Jefferson pair were playing it safe, banking on errors, but Jim scored on a stop-volley, and it was abruptly 40-15.

Match point.

Tod lashed a brilliant drive straight at Rocky, and Rocky lunged wildly at the ball. Just as it left his racket, an excited Jefferson fan let out a yell of mingled desperation and encouragement. The ball touched the tape, cakewalked maddeningly along the edge and dropped back into the West court.

Rocky was swept by a storm of pure fury. Match point, and just because some idiot felt like shooting his mouth off— He slammed his racket down on the court and strode across to the umpire's chair.

"Can't you keep the gallery quiet?" he shouted. "Yelling like Indians in the middle of my shots—"

"You'd already hit the ball," said the umpire, mopping his face and not looking any too pleased with life himself. He did, however, lift his hand and make a vague gesture toward the Jefferson crowd.

"*Tell* them to shut up," Rocky snapped. "Don't just wave your hand around."

"When I want your advice," said the umpire coldly, "I'll ask for it. Go back to your place, please."

Shaking with anger and feeling as if wasps were swarming inside his head, Rocky went back. He crashed down on the ball in a murderous serve that nearly split its seams, and it blasted its way into the net.

He spun the ball high for the second service and struck down on it again with the sharp satisfaction of physical violence. The savage zing of connecting ball and strings vibrated in the sudden silence that fell over the crowd.

Rocky's second serve, like the first, drove dead into the net.

"Double fault," said the umpire. "Deuce."

It was the break the twins had needed. They took the next two points, then settled down to annex the set, 9 to 7. Rocky's head was still swimming with anger and Jim was playing as if he'd broken a spring. All the zip had gone out of him.

"Game and set to the Andrews brothers," said the umpire. "One-all. Because of the heat, I'm authorizing a short rest."

Rocky joined Jim at the sidelines. "First sensible thing the guy's done today," he muttered. "I'd like to kick that high chair of his right out from under him."

Jim, kneeling to re-tie a shoelace, didn't answer and didn't look up.

Rocky glanced down at him. Jim's hands on the lace

were shaking, and there was a sharp white ridge of strain showing along the line of his jaw.

Rocky had a quick sense of discomfort. It hadn't occurred to him that the heat and the crowd might be getting on Jim's nerves, too. He said defensively, "He ought to keep the crowd quiet. That's his job."

Jim looked up. "The service was your job," he said. "You blew match point just because you were sore."

Rocky opened his mouth to retort and then it dawned on him that Jim was right. He had double-faulted at the most critical moment of the match, only because he'd been sore and wanted to hit something and hit it hard. He looked at Jim again. "Well, I'm—sorry," he said grudgingly.

Jim got to his feet and picked up his racket. "You're always sorry—afterwards," he said. "It's a bit late, isn't it?"

Rocky stared. "Well, it wasn't my fault that guy yelling upset me. I'm not easy-going like you are, Jim. You're not temperamental. Can I help it if I—"

Jim looked at him levelly. "Have you ever tried to help it?" he asked, and turned on his heel.

The Andrews twins were waiting in their places as Rocky walked slowly back to the baseline. Jim was standing near the alley and Rocky, looking at him quickly, felt a sharp stab of remorse. Jim really did look played out.

Well, they would have to win, that was all, and he would have to do what he could to take the load off Jim's shoulders and make it up to him. Jim was right. That double fault had been a fool exhibition. It made him responsible in a way. But was it his fault if—?

Tod Andrews' serve interrupted his thoughts. He spun the ball back to Dick's court, and Dick drove it hard down the alley line. Jim retrieved it smoothly, but there was no wrist snap in the return and the ball dropped too lightly. Dick tagged the baseline and took the point, and they were back on the seesaw. Point to West. Point to Jefferson. 30-15. 30-all.

Deuce. Deuce. Deuce.

Rocky's head began to ache. His shirt clung wetly to his shoulders, and his legs felt stiff and weighted. With Jim's sharp court game softened from weariness, the Andrews were getting better openings, and Rocky found himself tearing in frantic pursuit of their placements. On top of that, the birdbrain in the Jefferson front row had begun yelping his delight again.

Shut up, Rocky kept saying between his teeth. Shut up, shut up, shut up.

Two games to one for Jefferson. Then Jim scored a service ace, and they slugged their way up to deuce and took the game, only to lose the next when Tod Andrews put on a service exhibition of his own that ripped the court at their feet.

Jim drove a liner into the net, shook his head hard and walked away from the line. Rocky caught his eye. "Sorry," said Jim. There was a deep furrow between his eyebrows.

Rocky glowered resentfully at the sun. They *had* to win.

But they lost the next point on a floater that nestled just out of Rocky's reach. If he'd been fresh, he might have tagged it, but on both sides of the net now the brilliance and sparkle had gone out of the play. It was a matter of grimly, doggedly, getting the ball back across the net. They slugged it out endlessly, and finally it was four games even.

Rocky's feet dragged, and his mind went back wearily to that moment in the second set when they held match point. If he hadn't double-faulted then, he and Jim would be City champions now. If he'd kept his temper—

The sun was hotter than ever, and the crowd was bouncing around like a gang of Mexican jumping beans, only jumping beans were silent. These guys kept sounding off like firecrackers. Confound that umpire!

15-40, in favor of Rocky and Jim.

Rocky's nerves jerked tight. He flung himself with a savage surge of energetic hope at a drive that flickered across his vision and smashed it to Tod's feet. Tod whipped the ball back, straight down the center line and deep. Too deep. It was outside by a fraction of an inch, and Rocky's racket checked in mid-swing.

"In," said the umpire. "Thirty-forty."

Rocky spun on his heel. "That was *out!*"

"In," said the umpire, and gestured to him to get on with the game.

Rocky looked at Jim. "Was that ball in or out?" he demanded.

"Out the way I saw it," Jim said tiredly, "but the umpire's the boss."

Rocky turned back to the umpire and gave him a look that would have withered an oak tree. "That ball was out."

The umpire said, "That ball was in, and I'm the umpire here. Get on with the game."

Jim put a hand on Rocky's elbow and pushed him toward his own court. "It's no use arguing, Rocky. He has to call 'em the way he sees 'em."

Rocky jerked away, anger rolling up inside him like a black cloud. Of all the raw decisions! That ball had been out a mile, and if they thought he was just going to stand there calmly—

All the old familiar symptoms of anger began to rise inside him—nerves stretched to the snapping point, the feeling inside his head that was like smoke rising to choke him, the blind fury that made him want to hit out at whatever was nearest. And this time he was completely justified. Even Jim knew that ball had been out.

"Get on with the game, please," said the umpire.

Rocky strode angrily back to position. He was so furious that even the sun didn't seem hot any more. It was like having a fire inside, a fire that was fed by the knowledge he was in the right.

He swung his racket, slashing at the air, and then realized that Jim was looking at him.

Oh, the blazes with Jim and Jim's criticisms and Jim's superiority! Why shouldn't a guy get sore? Why shouldn't he blow up? Could he help it if his nerves were strung on wires? Could he help it if—

Suddenly, uncomfortably, he heard the echo of Jim's voice, "Have you ever tried to help it?"

Well, maybe not. But people were different. Some people were more temperamental than others, more—

Have you ever tried to help it?

The answer was no. Just like that—a flat, unequivocal no. He had never in his life tried to help it, never

tried to control the blazing upsurge of temper that was
making his head swim now. He remembered Jim's
words again, "You're always sorry—afterwards."

But what was he supposed to do about the way he
felt? This was a physical thing, this pounding inside
his head and the pressure of anger. He had to let it rip
or blow up. Even if Jim didn't care what the umpire
had done—

Jim did care, of course. You only had to look at the
set of his jaw now to know that.

If he blew now, he'd be letting Jim down again. It
would be one thing to lose the match because they were
overtired or outplayed. But it would be quite another
thing to lose it for the same reason they'd lost that second set: because Rocky Turner couldn't put a cork on
his temper.

He drew a deep breath. He stood there, with his
racket dangling, and he forced himself to be quiet long
enough for the tension to leave his muscles and the fog
of anger to drift out of his head. He forced himself to
concentrate intelligently on what he would do when
Tod's serve came over the net toward him.

The service, beautifully paced, flattened out in
Rocky's court. His racket spun accurately in the air,
catching sunlight on the handle, and took the ball
smoothly and crisply.

Tod, failing to allow for the coolly calculated top-
spin, drove his return into the net.

"Game," said the umpire. "Five-four in favor of Turner and Ellis."

Jim touched Rocky's shoulder as they passed. "Good
guy, Rocky," he said.

Rocky grinned. "Bet that one really hurt the ump."

Walking back to serve, he felt as if a ton of lead had been eased from his shoulders. Funny, that grin had felt perfectly natural and easy, and only a moment before he'd been in one of the hottest rages he'd ever known. He wasn't even irritated any more. He'd not only packed his anger away but he was sitting on the lid.

He had never known you could do that with your own feelings, put them away in mothballs and keep them there. It was an entirely new and victorious sensation, and he liked it.

He looked at Jim again and found Jim looking at him. Rocky realized suddenly that Jim knew exactly what had been going on. Come right down to it, maybe Jim went through that fight with himself every time the breaks went against *him*. Maybe everybody did. Maybe the difference was just the way you acted about it, whether you choked it down or whether you went all prima donna.

"Hey!" said Rocky, having made a discovery.

His serve sailed off the face of his racket. The return was to Jim's alley, and Jim raced back for the shot. The lead was out of his shoes now, and his hit was hard and clean. Dick blocked the return at the net, and Rocky sent back a dink shot to his feet. 15-love.

The crowd was squirming with excitement, and Rocky's pet peeve in the Jefferson front row was letting off steam vocally, pinch-hitting for a siren.

Rocky served a let that nicked the tape, then his second serve curved deceptively and Tod lofted it. Jim, at the net, smashed down on the ball from his fullest stretch and it exploded at the service line, bounding high out of Tod's grasping reach.

The twins took the next point, while the gallery hung breathless on every stroke. 30-15. Then 30-all. Rocky's jaw stiffened.

It was Jim's clockwork forehand that ended the next rally. The umpire said, "Match point."

Rocky, winded by the rally, went back to serve with his heart pounding against his ribs. Match point. This time he had to make it stick. He drew a deep breath and lifted his hand to spin the ball skyward.

A voice broke the stillness of waiting. "Double-fault it again!" yelled the voice. It was, inevitably, the Jefferson supporter in the front row.

Rocky turned his head toward the shout. "My public," he announced cheerfully. Then he faced the net, and the ball left his hand in a high arc of flight. His racket flashed up, then down. There was the sharp twang of accurately hit strings.

The ball sung over the center line—a service ace.

"Game, set and match," said the umpire.

The Andrews twins ran up to the net, hands outstretched, and Rocky and Jim—City champions— went to meet them. Maybe no one knew it except Jim and himself, but there had been two matches played that afternoon. And both times Rocky had been on the winning side.

Not bad for a guy with temperament.

MASTER MIND

IF IT HAD happened to anyone but Irish Mehaffey, maybe it wouldn't have been so crazy.

Irish is the fullback of the Kent High School football team, and he is a nice guy and a great back but very, very dumb. He weighs close to two hundred pounds and has bright yellow hair that stands up like a starched cornfield. We like him fine, but, as I say, he is not the intellectual type.

Now, I don't consider a knowledge of Greek or calculus essential to a fullback, but there is one thing that is essential and, as captain and quarterback of the team, I got pretty worried about it.

Irish couldn't learn signals. You could work out a foolproof system, and then along would come Irish and the backfield would knit itself up like an antimacassar, the ball would travel west and Irish would set off east into the rising sun. It wasn't good.

Finally, one afternoon in practice, he really distinguished himself and crashed into his own center. A second-string player picked up the resulting fumble and ran for a touchdown. In a regular game, it would have been simple murder.

That was when I called Chippy Martin into consultation. Chippy is editor of the Kent Weekly and he is fascinated by psychology. He looked at Irish thoughtfully and then said, "The trouble with you, Irish, is you don't concentrate."

"I don't?" said Irish.

"He doesn't even think," I said gloomily.

"Quiet, please.—Now, Irish, listen. The human mind is capable of practically anything. All of us vastly underestimate our capacities. The subconscious, for instance, is a controlling force which we seldom use. Do you ever use your subconscious, Irish?"

Irish said cautiously that he wasn't sure he had one. Chippy laid his face in his hands for a moment, but came up swinging. "Exactly. You *don't* use it, and it is a great imponderable force." He stopped off to translate "imponderable," and then went on, reeling off a lot of lovely textbook words. I left them alone, certain it would do no good but willing to try anything once, if it would help the Mehaffey subconscious.

The next day, in practice, a miracle happened. Irish ran through signal drills like a veteran. I was stunned but as happy as a bookworm in a one-volume encyclopedia, and I patted Irish on the back exuberantly. He looked at me rather oddly. "It seems to work, doesn't it?" he said.

I said that, whatever it was, it worked fine and to keep it up.

"I don't understand it, Jerry," Irish said, "but

Chippy says it's a matter of concentration. It's kind of peculiar."

"You just go on being peculiar that way."

He shook his head and said he hoped it was all right. All right? It was wonderful.

Then came Peabody High. I knew in the first ten minutes that Peabody was going to give us a fight. A pint-sized halfback named Jimmy Alfeo ran forty yards, winding up nice and cozy in our end zone. They converted, and it was seven points for Peabody. We settled down to respecting Alfeo and put a cork in that gentleman's activities, so they started smacking us from end to end. This fine offensive frenzy was rough on their center who was blocking his ears off, and when we got the ball I threw Irish right at him. It was payday for Mehaffey, and he picked up enough yardage to squat us in enemy territory. A pass did the rest, and we scored, tying the game up, 7-7, when the ball sailed over the crossbar. This irked Peabody, and they started tossing the book at us, but we got cagey and play bogged down.

Then, with six minutes to go in the game, Peabody's full bucked almost to midfield again. Two long passes got their ears pinned back, and on fourth down they were on their own forty-six with no future. We spread to receive the inevitable kick.

I went back to safety, and I happened to glance at Irish. He had a most peculiar expression, sort of far-away and baffled as if he was listening to voices, but there wasn't anything to hear. I shrugged and waited for the kick.

All of a sudden, Irish started waving his arms around

and yelling for time out. I said to myself, "He's sat
on a bee," which was silly because he wasn't sitting and
autumn isn't bee-time. But I figured, insects or no insects, desperation had set in, so I signaled the referee.

Irish came racing over like a trumpeting elephant
and grabbed me with both hands. "Jerry!" he yelped.
"They're going to try a pass!"

I said, "Are you crazy?" Risking a pass, with the
score tied and Peabody in its own home state, would be
just the kind of thing that sets the squirrels looking for
nuts. I said again, good and exasperated, "Irish, are
you crazy?"

He shook his head. He looked kind of solemn. "No.
They're planning a Statue of Liberty."

For a moment, I thought he'd played too much ball
in too much sun. Then he suddenly shook his head as
if he was getting gnats out of his ears. "Gee, I'm sorry,
Jerry," he said. "I just had a sort of—hunch, or something. I guess I'm screwy."

I guessed so too, but I whacked him on the shoulder
and told him everything was all right and he went back
into position. The whistle shrilled. I got all set to catch
the punt and figured that with good blocking I might
be able to put us in shooting distance for a field goal.
I waited.

It was a pass.

It was the Statue of Liberty, that gray-bearded, sec-
ond-cousin-to-Methuselah, old Liberty play. Alfeo
sparked it. We were caught as flat as a pancake under
a steamroller.

The scoreboard said Peabody 13, Kent 7. And we
never got it back.

I walked home very slowly. If I had played Irish's crazy hunch, we'd have ended with at least a tie. But what quarterback in his senses was going to look for a pass out of a set-up like that? I took a deep breath but it didn't do any good, and then I heard footsteps behind me. It was Irish and Chippy.

Chippy said, "Irish told me, Jerry. About the pass."

I said, "Oh."

Chippy poked Irish. "Tell him what happened, Irish."

"I don't know what happened." Irish looked bewildered. "I was just standing there, Jerry, waiting for the kick, and I didn't have to concentrate on you because there weren't going to be any signals, and so I just happened to concentrate on the Peabody quarterback, and—"

"And?" Chippy prompted.

"And all of a sudden," Irish said unhappily, "it was just like being tuned in on a radio set and I knew he was going to call the pass."

I gulped. Chippy looked at me and nodded very slowly. "That's it, Jerry," he said in an awed voice. "Irish is telepathic."

I said, "That's nonsense!" I think I shouted it.

Chippy reached out a hand and made me stop walking. "Irish," he said, "what's Jerry thinking about now?"

Irish looked at me, and you could see wheels going around in his head. "He's thinking that maybe he's got sunstroke and he'd better go somewhere and have a coke."

I leapt like a porcupine that's sat on one of its own

quills. It was perfectly true. I stared at Irish, and I think my teeth were chattering.

Chippy stared at me. "See what I mean?"

I saw. There was no question about it. Kent High School had a telepathic fullback.

Well, of course, in a way it was wonderful. After all, we knew every play before it came, and the sportswriters called us "the team with the sixth sense." But there was one thing that wasn't wonderful, and that was the way it affected Irish. Every day he got sadder and sadder and his piledriver line plunges lost a lot of their power. But it didn't matter. We won anyway. The miracle team. The year's sensation. The big Green wave. We couldn't go wrong.

Then, the day before the big game of the season against Pike High, the bottom fell out.

Pike is tradition. If we beat Pike, it doesn't matter what happens the rest of the year, and the corridors at Kent were plastered with signs reading, "Take a poke at Pike," "Make Pikers out of Pike," and "Pike's Peak or Bust."

I was not prepared for what happened.

It was ten o'clock at night and I had just crawled into bed when the doorbell rang. Pop yelled upstairs at me, "Hey, Jerry! Irish wants to see you," and I battled my way into my bathrobe and went down. Irish was sitting on the living room couch.

"What are you doing here?" I asked. "You're supposed to be in bed."

He put his head in his hands. "I know.—Jerry, I'm resigning from the team."

I felt as if someone had pulled the room out from under me. "You're *what?*"

"Resigning from the team." He looked like one of those hound dogs that practically burst into tears if you speak to them. "I can't possibly go on playing for Kent·with things like this. It isn't—it isn't— What's the word for it?"

All of a sudden, I knew what the word was that he wanted. Maybe it had been kicking around at the back of my mind too. It wasn't ethical to use a telepathic fullback.

"That's the word," said Irish. "Ethical."

I hadn't said it. He'd heard it crashing around in my head. It was unsettling. It was more than unsettling, because, now that I honestly thought of it, it certainly wasn't ethical, and, in that case, what were we going to do? Play Pike without a fullback?

I needed reinforcements, and I walked over to the phone and called Chippy Martin. When I finally got him awake enough to tell him what had happened, there was a short stunned silence. Then he said, "I'll come right over. Just be calm, Jerry. Be perfectly calm."

He was a fine one to go around telling people to be calm. When he came in, he was wearing two unmatched shoes, his kid brother's raincoat and his father's hat. The raincoat sleeves came to his elbows, and the hat came to his chin.

"Irish," said Chippy, even before he got through the door, "you can't *do* this to us. It isn't ethical."

It wasn't a very good choice of words, and, after a minute, Chippy could see it for himself. Irish was perfectly right. We couldn't argue with him. I went out into the kitchen and got some bananas and cookies and we just sat, moody as three black crows, and chewed.

After a while, Chippy said, "There's some way out of this. We can't possibly replace you, Irish.—Look, can you play without being telepathic?"

"Huh?" said Irish, rather thickly. He had just peeled his third banana.

Chippy elaborated. "I mean, you only get the other team's plays when you concentrate on the quarterback, don't you? Suppose you concentrated on someone else, like me on the sidelines, then what do you think would happen?"

"I'd know what you were thinking. Like now. You're thinking I'm eating too many bananas and that I'm an awful nuisance and you wish you were home in bed."

Chippy winced. "I don't think you're a nuisance, Irish," he said hastily, "and you can have all the bananas you want. They can pop out at your ears, for all I care. Please stop concentrating on me."

After this outburst, he sat still for a moment. "Well, if you thought about me during the game, you'd be all right, wouldn't you?"

Irish said cautiously, "I don't know. I might just accidentally start thinking about the quarterback, and then—"

"Then you'd know the play," I said.

Irish nodded miserably and reached for another banana. I put a cookie in his hand instead, before he started climbing trees and asking for coconuts.

"Well, in that case," said Chippy, "keep it to yourself."

Irish looked at him. "You mean, even if I know what's going to happen, I just stand there and don't tell Jerry?"

"Exactly. When our team's got the ball, you concentrate on Jerry. And, when Pike's got the ball, concentrate on me."

Irish gulped. I gulped. After a moment, Chippy gulped but that was his banana. He wasn't a football player and he didn't see all the difficulties ahead. Still, it was worth trying. I stood up. "You go home to bed, Irish, and forget about this. All you have to do tomorrow is lug that ball. See?"

"I see," said Irish. He sounded as happy and buoyant as a sick clam.

Chippy got up and put on his father's hat. His ears disappeared. "Look," said Chippy, his worst suspicions confirmed. "I've lost weight."

I pushed them both out the door, and then I staggered back to bed.

It didn't rain for the Pike game. The sun came out and the sky was blue and life was one grand sweet song. Or ought to have been. The way I felt, it could just as well have been raining Maltese kittens and St. Bernards.

We had scouted Pike pretty thoroughly. They had a fine team, powerful and fast. Their quarterback, Joe Nesbitt, had quite a reputation, and their ends were flypaper on passes. I knew we'd need Irish to tighten the line and pull them in. I wanted to be able to mix the plays and use everything we had. This was *the* game. I looked at Irish. He was buckling his helmet and talking to himself. I had never seen Irish talking to himself before, and it made me nervous. I went over and touched his arm, and he jumped like I'd hit him with a cactus. "Oh, hello, Jerry," he said wanly.

"What were you talking about, Irish?"

"Me?" said Irish. "Peter Piper picked a peck of pickled peppers, a peck of pickled peppers——"

I clutched him. "Irish!"

"Huh?"

"Don't *do* that!"

He looked at me reproachfully. "But I have to concentrate on something, Jerry, and Peter Piper helps me keep my mind off Joe Nesbitt and what he's thinking."

"I thought you were concentrating on Chippy."

He shook his head. "I tried that. He thinks too fast. First it's the weather, and then it's the game, and then he starts writing an article in his head, and I get all confused. I thought Peter Piper would clear things up."

I shook my head—it was a fine day for head-shaking—and went back into position with my knees playing reveille. We won the toss and elected to receive. It was a beautiful boot, end-over-end, and I pulled it in on the fifteen and started uptown behind good crisp blocking. Irish took his man out cleanly—him and Peter Piper. I began to feel better, and I hit the thirty-eight before I was stopped.

An end run picked up eight yards, and we were knocking at the midfield door. I called Irish on an off-tackle play and he made the down. I gave him the nod again, and he blasted the Pike line for another first.

The Kent stands began to shriek. We pulled a reverse and it was like taking candy from a baby. First again, on the Pike thirteen.

"We want a touchdown," yelled the stands. We couldn't miss.

We didn't. In three plays, Irish whammed the ball straight through and, on the last one, he went over the line. Six points for Kent, and the game barely started. I felt colossal. We converted, and Pike was seven in the hole. It was Christmas, and Santa was stuffing our stocking.

Joe Nesbitt returned our kick to the thirty-eight. Two line plunges netted about seven yards. I took another look at Irish, and suddenly I saw him straighten up and look wildly around him. He knows the play, I thought.

Well, so did I. We covered for a pass.

We covered, but the pass was good anyhow. Pike had a first down on our forty-seven, and I could see Irish's lips moving. Pike's next pass was incomplete and nearly intercepted; they tried once more and kicked into the end zone.

That threat had failed. We took the ball on our twenty, and got ready to roll. But Pike was steadying, and what was more they had an eye on Irish. He made about two inches, and then we were set back five yards for an offside. I kicked, and it was first and ten for Pike on their forty-four. They came up over the ball very fast and hit a stone wall. Then the left half found a hole and scuttled through for twelve. A pass was complete on our thirty, and the receiver added seven yards before he was stopped.

Irish's face was all screwed up. He'd known it was coming. I winced all the way through, from helmet to cleats. Joe Nesbitt passed laterally. The half fumbled, and Irish pounced, recovering.

Happy days! I thought. Irish couldn't have known the guy would fumble, so it was heads-up playing that did that one for us, not telepathy. I saw Irish beaming, for a change.

But they slapped our wrists again and we made five yards in three tries and kicked out of trouble. At least, we thought we were out of trouble. Joe Nesbitt had his own notions and hiked to the forty-seven. First and ten. They pulled a cute play, a fake pass and a run to our weak side. Irish did a funny thing on that one. He started to drive in, suddenly stopped and just stood, looking helpless, with his hands spread wide.

It was almost a twenty-five yard run. I called for time out and went over to Irish. It was like I thought; he'd known the play, blew in to break it up, realized suddenly he wasn't supposed to know it and stopped practically in mid-air.

This was going to be lovely. I told him to pick out a clover or something on the field and concentrate on that. He said, "Yes, Jerry" very meekly, and then added, "Which clover?" I hit my forehead with my hand and told him to go back to concentrating on Chippy. However confused Chippy's thoughts were, they couldn't be any worse than what was happening.

Pike was rolling. It took them two shots to reach our ten. We stiffened and threw them for a two-yard loss, and then their right half wrecked everything with an

end run. He downed the ball back of our goal posts, and
it was 7-6.

They tied it up in a bowknot on the kick. The quarter ended 7-7.

In the second quarter, we played on the seesaws.
Irish was lousy, a word which my English teacher says
he deplores, but if he will find me another word for
what Irish was I'll be happy to use it. You could see
what was happening to the poor guy. He was always
concentrating on the wrong thing at the wrong time,
and it must have been like chasing ants at a picnic. You
scoop them out of the hot dogs and they turn up in the
thermos bottle. I started longing for the good old days
when nothing had been wrong with Irish except a
genius for mixing signals.

Then, in trouble again on our own twenty-two, we
quick-kicked. Joe Nesbitt fielded and, like a little gentleman, he fumbled. We recovered by a miracle and
were set up in scoring territory once more. I dropped
back for a long pass, it settled like a homing pigeon, and
the end stepped over the line without a finger laid on
him.

The try for goal was short, but the score was 13-7 in
our favor.

In the third quarter, Pike took to the air and camped
twice in scoring territory but we kicked out of danger.
Then an awful thing happened.

With about five seconds to go in the quarter, Nesbitt
squirmed and fought his way into the secondary. The
play had exploded out of a lateral and caught all of us
off balance, including Irish who had undoubtedly been
concentrating perfectly legally on a clover. I saw a

startled look spread across Irish's face, and then I saw him spin and start after Nesbitt. Now, Nesbitt is fast, but Irish was coming in on an angle and, by all the laws of mathematics, physics and luck, he had a good chance to cut Nesbitt off his feet.

But Irish slowed down. I actually saw him doing it. His feet stopped hitting the turf and his hands stopped reaching. When he made the tackle, he was wide out, and his shoulder struck air. Joe Nesbitt didn't even have to shrug to clear him; Joe Nesbitt just kept on running.

Kent 13, Pike 13. I called time out, stalked over to Irish and shook him. "You crazy loon," I sputtered, "what happened to you?"

Irish stared at me. I gave him another shake, like a malted milk. "He's faster than I am," said Irish.

"Who's faster than you?" I yelled.

"Nesbitt."

"Who says he's faster?"

"*He* said so," said Irish, as if that explained everything.

"What do you mean, *he* said so? He didn't say anything—he was running, which was what you should have been doing too."

Irish looked at me forlornly, and then he looked at the ground. "He was thinking about it," Irish muttered. "He was running hard and he was thinking he was faster than I was, and I heard him thinking it and I knew he was right, and so I guess I—I just— Jerry, I'm resigning from the team right now!"

All I knew for certain was that there was nobody to replace him. "Look, Irish," I said firmly, "you've got to stay in. There's only one quarter left in the game." I shut my eyes tight and prayed for strength. "Now, listen," I said, "this sounds crazy, but do it anyway. When we've got the ball, concentrate on me. When we haven't got the ball, just don't think at all. See?"

"But—" said Irish.

"Don't think at all," I repeated. "And don't try to do anything. Just get out of the way. Don't try to make a tackle, don't back up the line. *Just get out of the way.*"

He looked at me. I guess he thought I was crazy. I knew I was, but I couldn't see any other answer. He'd be all right on offense if he concentrated on me, because I'd know what he should be doing. But I couldn't nurse him along on defense, never knowing what to expect, and I figured the only safe thing was for him to keep his paws off the whole business. I said, "Don't argue, Irish. Do what I tell you."

He said, "Yes." He didn't have the slightest intention of arguing.

Time out ended, and we lined up for the kick. The stands stopped breathing. Then the whistle shrilled, and Nesbitt booted the pigskin. It lifted in the air, hung for a second over the crossbar and dropped, safe—14 to 13 for Pike as the quarter ended.

The fourth quarter was most peculiar. Irish did just what I'd told him to; he concentrated on me so hard when we had the ball that his ears must have been stiff, and he never missed a signal. The only trouble was that Pike, with its one-point lead, had no intention of giving ground.

Time ticked its way out. The clock showed two minutes to go. A sequence of running plays found us near
midfield. I thought of a fake center buck and lateral
that we had been successful with a few times. It was
worth trying. If it flopped, we still had time for a
couple of passes that might click.

I called signals. I could almost feel Irish concentrating on me, and I had the consolation of knowing
that, anyway, he would get the signals right. The ball
was snapped.

And, too late, something clicked in my mind and I
saw the play I should have called, the play I would
have called if my brain hadn't been all wound up with
Irish's. There was a hole big enough to drive a truck
through between defensive right tackle and guard. If
I had shot a double spinner at that hole, Irish would
be on his way.

And then I saw, too late again, what I had done by
thinking about the spinner play. Half of me had di-
rected the fake center buck; half of me was mourning
over a double spinner that could have been. And, poor
Irish, concentrating on both halves, was a split person-
ality.

Completely lost, he tucked the ball under his arm
and ran toward me.

I fled. He chased me. The whole Pike team chased
him. I raced for the sidelines. I wanted to tunnel my
way under the nearest bench and disappear forever,
but some reasonable instinct turned me downfield.
One lone thought wavered in my shattered brain. I
knew I mustn't run toward our own goalposts. "The
other goal," I thought. "The other goal!" And then I

simply rolled up like an embattled hedgehog and removed myself from the scene.

Irish didn't follow me, because I'd rolled without
thinking about it. He was following my mind, not my
legs, and my mind was fixed on Pike's goal line.

It wasn't football; that much I'm sure of. It may
have been baseball, or water polo. Tiddleywinks, perhaps. It looked like Waterloo. Irish beat a path down
the sidelines. Pike pounded after him. I never did
know what became of our boys; I guess they just decided to faint in their tracks.

With the Kent stands screaming, Irish stampeded
over the Pike forty-yard line, the thirty, the twenty—
A Pike runner came up out of nowhere. On the ten, he
drew level with Irish. On the three, he hit him. The
bleachers rocked with the concussion; I think a couple
of clouds fell out of the sky.

Irish fell face down with a mighty thud, stretching
for the last precious inch. He wasn't over the goal line.

But the ball was. Kent 19, Pike 14.

He was dazed when he finally sat up, and he was
rubbing his head. He said, "What happened?"

I told him. My own head was singing a victory chant
and the sun was as bright as firecrackers. I told him
what had happened, how first I'd signalled one play
and then thought of another and how he'd mixed them
together and gone mad. I told him that he'd won the
game for Kent.

Irish looked at me crossly and shook his head hard.
"What's the trouble with you, Jerry? You're talking

through your hat. How could I possibly know what you were thinking?"

I looked at him, and I tried to be calm. It must have been the crack on his head, I thought, and no doubt Chippy would have eighty-two fancy names to explain it. But, whatever it was, Irish Mehaffey, our telepathic fullback, was telepathic no more.

So that's the story. Chippy said that if I wrote it all out on paper it might clear my mind and I'd stop having nightmares.

In the meantime, if anyone can suggest some way to make a fullback learn how to memorize signals, they may write me a letter, outlining their theories. The address is Kent High School.

TRIPLE THREAT

"MY FRIENDS," said Glen Harris, putting his hands on the table and leaning forward persuasively to fix his roommates with a penetrating gaze, "can we any longer ignore the implications? Can we go blindly along, pretending— For Pete's sake, watch what you're doing with that javelin!"

Speed Holloway innocently lowered eight and a half feet of steel-tipped wood, and looked wonderingly at Glen. "I'm not doing anything," he said in an injured voice.

"Not doing anything?" Glen echoed indignantly. "Merely trying to assassinate me, that's all. Not doing anything! It's—it's—"

"Murderous assault with a lethal weapon." Mickey Mullane crawled out from under his desk where he had been chasing a pencil. "What you want is a policeman. Meadows, send out for a policeman and some soda crackers." He took an absent-minded bite out of the pencil and glared at the sheet of paper before him.

115

"Look, if you came into your room and found a leopard under the sofa, what would you do?"

"Have my eyes examined," said Glen, taking up his stand safely across the room from the javelin wielder. "Can we go blindly along, pretending—" he began again, then paused. "Now look what you've done—you and your wild cats. What was I talking about?"

"Leopards! Leopards!" Mickey insisted. "This is serious. It's the turning point of the first act of this play I'm writing. A crisis has been reached."

"I wish you'd shut up," said Glen plaintively. "You don't seem to realize that the debate comes off Wednesday night."

"*You* don't seem to realize," said Mickey urgently, "that the leopard is already under the sofa. No next Wednesday night about it. Are you going to leave me sitting here with a full-grown leopard under the sofa?"

"Get a mousetrap," Speed suggested, balancing the javelin lightly and studying the grip of his fingers with rapt interest.

"Take an aspirin," said Glen, "Maybe it's just a little pussycat after all. What do you think, Speed?"

"I'm sure it is," said Speed amiably. "What would a leopard be doing under a sofa anyhow?"

Mickey seized the opening. "Well, you see it was this way. This man—"

"What man?"

"The one who lives in this house—"

"What house?"

"The one where the leopard is."

"WHAT LEOPARD?" This in chorus from both his companions.

Mickey tottered to his feet and, transporting himself tenderly across the room, lay down on the couch with a newspaper over his face. "Leave me, gentlemen," he whispered. "I need rest and quiet."

Speed hurdled a chair casually and sat on Mickey's legs. "Rest from what?" he inquired cynically.

Mickey reared upwards. "I'm the hardest working guy at Brewster Prep," he announced, "and probably if it wasn't for me, there wouldn't be a school at all. In fact, without me Brewster would be a howling oasis."

"Did you ever see an oasis howling?" Speed asked Glen.

Glen nodded. "There was one under our window last night," he said. "I threw a shoe at it, and it went away."

"Shuddup," Mickey requested. "The word I want for me is invaluable."

"We'll give it to you for Christmas," said Speed kindly. "What makes you think you're invaluable?"

"Well, what *would* Brewster do without me?" Mickey said, rolling over energetically. "I edit its newspaper, write its plays and songs and poems, keep it entertained and generally make myself indispensable. To say nothing of listening to Glen make speeches and watching you cavort around on the track team."

"Mere nothings," said Glen. "One debate for dear old Brewster is worth ten of your so-called plays—"

"And one heave of my trusty javelin or one record high jump is worth twenty editions of the Daily and—" Speed added unwisely, "thirty of Glen's speeches."

"Bah!" said Mickey and Glen in chorus.

"Well, wait and see what happens if we win the

State track meet," Speed prophesied. "Then we'll see who's famous."

"Wait and see what happens if our debating team goes into the national finals," said Glen.

"Wait and see what happens when I get my play written and produce it here and maybe win the Interscholastic prize," said Mickey, sitting up and waving his arms around triumphantly. "Boy! I'll bet I even get the Newton Cup for being the guy who's contributed most to the school."

"Ha," said Speed, picking up his javelin again and assuming his original position.

"Ha," said Glen, striking a pose and beginning to address an imaginary audience.

"He who ha's last," Mickey remarked, "ha's best. I don't like to boast, but I'll make you guys a bet that if any of us three gets the Newton Cup, it'll be yours very respectfully."

"It's a deal," said Speed. "My poor trusting innocent."

"Winner gets a steak dinner at Hart's," Glen suggested, "with trimmings. You're on."

Mickey collapsed against the sofa pillows with a sigh. "Waiter," he said soulfully, "make mine rare."

A few days later, Mickey, pursuing his educational career in his customary hasty fashion, cannoned off a classmate into a professor, and thence, with apologies all around, into the track coach.

The classmate and professor weighed but lightly on the Mullane conscience, but the coach was another matter altogether. The coach, in short, was a potential source of news, and one of the great unwritten laws of the Press is not to knock people down when they may have a story for you.

Mickey, therefore, picked up the coach's hat penitently and assumed the expression of a hopeful and trusting pelican waiting to be fed fish.

"In a hurry?" said the coach, dusting his hat off rather bitterly. "Why don't you come out for the hundred yard dash?"

Mickey ignored the bitterness and took the opening.

"Any dope on the team for tomorrow's colyum, sir?" he asked, feeling for a pencil and looking intensely professional. "I see where the Daily Tribune has picked Brewster to win the State title."

Coach Fletcher smiled wanly. "That's Joe Griggs' idea of it," he said, "and Joe's the type who does crossword puzzles in ink. A good guy, but a little too optimistic for a sportswriter." He rubbed his nose thoughtfully. "Did you know that Bud Ellingson's out of the pole vault?"

Mickey pointed like an Irish setter. "Gosh, no! What happened?"

"Sprained his wrist," said the coach laconically. "He's feeling very low."

"Poor kid," Mickey sympathized. "But, jeepers, who's going to take his place? Weren't you counting on him for a first?"

"The first rule of a coach," said Coach Fletcher, "is never to count on anything. Yes, I was." He sighed deeply. "It'll be up to Speed now, and he's got a busy afternoon ahead without that."

"He was entered in the pole vault anyhow, wasn't he?"

"Speed? Sure, he's entered for everything that hops, swims or flies. You know Speed. By the way, speaking of that gentleman—" He paused.

"Yerp?" said Mickey encouragingly.

"Speaking of that gentleman," the coach continued thoughtfully. "I wonder if you can't lend a helping hand. Speed's heading for a fall. He's developing as nice a case of over-confidence as I've ever had the pleasure of witnessing."

"Tsk," said Mickey inadequately.

"Tsk is right," the coach agreed. "He's got it all doped out. He's going to get a first in the century, the high jump and the broad jump. A second in the quarter mile and the javelin throw, and what's more—"

"Is there more?" said Mickey meekly.

"Stick around, my boy. This is educational." Coach Fletcher glared absently at a passing freshman. "What's more, he expects to place in the pole vault. He's practically won the meet for us before it begins."

"Cute," said Mickey. "Very cute."

"And I thought," said the coach hopefully, "that you might be able to take him down a few pegs in your usual—"

"—masterly fashion," Mickey finished for him. "It's as good as done, sir. Mullane, the balloon-pricker. But, confidentially, isn't it perfectly possible that Speed *will* get all those points? Think of last year."

"I am thinking of last year," said the coach sourly, "and I admit that Speed's improved since then. But—"

well, did you ever hear of Stan Rutherford of Colburn?"

"Rutherford of Colburn," Mickey mused. "Sounds like a movie title. Yes, sure, I've heard of him, sir. He was the guy that beat Timmy Parker out in the high hurdles, when Timmy figured it was all sewed up. Po' Timmy. That was a right sad day, suh."

"It was," the coach agreed. "The point is that Rutherford is better than ever this year, and it's only too likely that he'll walk away with the meet right under Speed's very nose."

"Is walking away with the meet anything like bringing home the bacon?" Mickey inquired. "Sorry, sorry, these things just come on me. What do you want me to do? Try to get it through Speed's cranium that the big bad wolf is a piker compared to Rutherford of Colburn? Ah, that name!"

Coach Fletcher nodded. "Use your own discretion."

Mickey beamed. "I have a wonderful discretion," he said brightly. "Good as new—hardly been used at all. Speed will love it."

"Oh, git!" said the coach in despair, and Mickey fled.

"Act One, Scene Two. The same evening." Mickey gazed thoughtfully at the sheet of paper he had just inserted into his typewriter, and took a large bite out of a convenient apple. "Enter two—"

"—submarines, cleverly disguised as ducks," said Glen, peering interestedly over his shoulder.

"Go 'way," Mickey muttered around the apple, making irritated gestures.

"Stop fuddling over that," said Glen, "and pay some attention to me. I'm having trouble."

"Good," Mickey commented callously, and typed in the word "policemen" before he went on. "Such as which?"

"Resolved," said Glen, "that the jury system should be abolished."

"What ever for?" Mickey inquired in some surprise. "What's the jury system done to you?"

"Don't be funny," said Glen, taking the rest of Mickey's apple and disposing of it in two large bites. "We're taking the affirmative side in the debate tomorrow night, and all my arguments are so old they've got whiskers. And we've gotta win—we've just gotta, or we won't go into the national finals."

"Stop chewing in my ear," Mickey suggested plaintively, fortunately not realizing that it was his apple that was being chewed.

"Can't you think of any interesting, unusual, arresting, convincing, brilliant approach to the subject?"

"Frankly, no," said Mickey, then swiveled around in his chair with a heartrending sigh. "You want me to listen to you speechify?" he asked gloomily.

Glen registered guilt. "Well, if you wouldn't mind — Just a few minutes— It helps a lot."

"Oke," said Mickey. "Only wait a second. I've got a question to propound to our old pal Speed." He crumpled a piece of paper into a nice wad and shot it across the room, catching Speed neatly on the ear. That gentleman, who had been slumbering peacefully on the couch, shot upwards with a howl.

"Who," said Mickey, without benefit of preamble, "is this guy Rutherford I hear so much about?"

"Who threw that?" said Speed, getting down to brass tacks.

"Rutherford of Colburn," Mickey repeated. "Who is he?"

"An athlete," said Speed, rubbing his ear vexedly. "He yumps. Did you wake me up just to ask me that fool question?"

"I didn't wake you up," Mickey said patiently. "It was the wad of paper. I was merely what is known as a contributing cause. And it isn't a fool question. I want to run an article on him in the Daily. From what I hear, he's tops."

"Oh, he's not so much," said Speed easily, rolling over and burying his nose in a pillow. "I can beat him in anything but the pole vault."

"Indeed, indeed?" Mickey said politely. "I hear he's done a hundred and sixty-eight in the javelin throw."

"So what?" said Speed. "I've done one seventy-two and better."

"And he's equaled the State record in the high jump."

"So've I."

"And 10:3 in the century," Mickey offered, beginning to be a little uncertain of his facts.

"I've shaded that," said Speed. "What you trying to do—scare me?"

"Oh, no. Of course not," Mickey exclaimed hastily. "I just wanted to write an article on him, that's all."

"Trying to convince me he's dangerous?" Speed chortled. "Mickey, my mutt, no one believes your articles but yourself." He pulled another pillow down over his head and effectively removed himself from the conversation.

"Well, that won't work," said Mickey under his breath. He scratched the tip of his nose, gazed upon Speed with a glassy eye, then began to type carefully in the center of the sheet of paper—"SEE JOE GRIGGS."

This he removed from the typewriter, folded and placed tenderly in his pocket.

"What's that for?" said Glen, interestedly.

"Important business engagement," Mickey told him. "Got to see a man about a monkey." He turned his attention to Glen, who was all but sitting up on his hind legs and begging to be allowed to declaim. "Go ahead," said Mickey resignedly.

"Mr. Chairman," said Glen, "honorable judges, and gentlemen. The question—"

"Aren't judges gentlemen?" Mickey interrupted.

Glen eyed him sternly. "Children," said Glen, "should be seen and not heard."

"Yessir," said Mickey meekly, and, casting one yearning glance at his typewriter, settled down to hear and criticize a vigorous attack on the jury system.

A few days later, Speed, giving a convincing imitation of a runaway locomotive, shot into the sacred office of the Brewster Daily News—"Read About Your School"—and seized the editor-in-chief with more force than formality.

"Listen," Speed demanded passionately, waving a

copy of the Daily Tribune under the editorial nose, "did you see this?"

"I can't even see it now," Mickey pointed out plaintively, taking a blue pencil from behind his ear and putting a professional O.K. on a piece of copy. "Hold still, you blithering idiot. What do you think I am—a whirling dervish?"

"Well, *read* it!" Speed yelped, waving the paper more frantically than ever.

Mickey took it from him gently but firmly, and opened it out on the table. "Probable showers followed by slowly rising temperatures," he read solemnly. "Think of that. Ambassador sails on eve of parley. Tsk, what *is* the world coming to? What will they do——"

Speed seized the paper and turned to the proper page. *"Will* you pay some attention?" he seethed indignantly. "Read that article by Joe Griggs. Read it, I ask you. What does he think he is?"

Mickey bent obediently over the article and read it through earnestly, although he had seen it twice already and several of the phrases were his own. "Rutherford," Mickey read disjointedly, "superior to opponents. Hmmmm. Probably outranks Brewster's flash, Speed Holloway. Well, well. Better than last year . . . sensational . . . sweep to victory. . . . Is the day of Brewster supremacy over? My, my, what a personal question!"

"Don't be funny," said Speed dejectedly. "I thought you were just talking through your hat about him. Is he really that good?"

"Who?" Mickey inquired innocently. "Oh, you

mean this Rutherford. Well, personally," he ventured
with caution, "I've never seen him, but Joe Griggs
doesn't generally go out on a limb unless he has some
reason to. Still, he may not be quite that good." His
tone managed to imply profound doubt of the pos-
sibility, and Speed's face dropped another inch.

"Golly," said Speed, in tones of hushed awe, "maybe
I can't beat him. Maybe we'll lose the meet."

"Oh, well," said Mickey airily. "What's a meet? By
the way, you might like to read the article I wrote on
the debate. It's good stuff." He took a modest and un-
authorized bow. "Glen did himself proud, if I do say
so. Must've been my fancy flights of criticism."

"He's done 10:1 in the hundred-yard dash," said
Speed.

"Glen has?" Mickey said incredulously. "I don't believe it."

"Oh, *don't* be funny!" Speed wailed. "This is serious."

Mickey sat down and put his feet on the table.
"After all," said Mickey brightly, "it's three weeks
before the meet. Who knows? Maybe you can do ten in
the hundred. It's only a few seconds faster than you're
running it now."

"Only!" Speed groaned.

"And surely an inch or two in the high jump isn't
much," Mickey hinted delicately.

"Why not a foot while you're at it?" Speed inquired
bitterly.

"A foot would be safer," Mickey agreed kindly. He
returned his own feet to the floor, gave his type-

writer a jerk and gazed fondly at the sheet of paper in it. "Act One, Scene Two," it read. "Enter two policemen, carrying guns."

"Well," said Mickey, "I wouldn't worry about it. It will all work out some way." He began to type. "First Policeman (nervously) : Are you—"

"Are you just going to sit there and type," said Speed unbelievingly, "when my whole future is falling around me in ruins?"

"It's your socks," Mickey retorted unsympathetically, "and you could correct that by wearing garters."

"Listen," Speed begged pitifully, leaning over the typewriter and obscuring the struggling policemen. "Come out to the field with me and clock me in the quarter mile. Maybe there's something I'm not doing right in the pole vault. *What* did Griggs say he'd done in the high jump?"

"Relax," Mickey advised. "You're getting feverish. It's kinetic energy you need, or something. I read about it somewhere."

"What do you mean—kinetic energy?" Speed demanded hollowly. "What I need is comfort and sustainment and someone to clock me."

A look of longing came into Mickey's eyes, and he stroked his typewriter tenderly.

"Why don't you work out with me?" said Speed suddenly. "Exercise would do you good—you're not a bad runner and you could learn to jump."

"I don't want to learn to jump," said Mickey, putting a cover over the typewriter and getting to his feet. "I once read a horrible story about a boy who practised jumping fifteen hours a day, and one morning he got up and looked into the mirror, and what do you think he saw?"

"What?" said Speed, unwisely.

"His reflection," said Mickey. "Come on. I'll clock you. I'll run around the track with you. I'll even let you throw a javelin at me. Mickey, the Stooge." He patted his typewriter with fond regret. "Farewell, my lovely," he said mournfully. "C'mon, Speed."

Mickey collapsed on a bench in the locker room and panted like an overstuffed grampus. Coach Fletcher dropped beside him and looked sympathetically inquiring.

"I'm going to send you a bill," said Mickey darkly, between gasps, "for damages. I'm a mental, physical and spiritual wreck. The only thing he doesn't make me do with him is the hundred-yard dash. I'm permitted just to stand by and time that, as a special treat. Did you see us doing the quarter mile?"

"No," said the coach gravely.

"He met me coming back," said Mickey, "twice. I don't claim to be a great athlete, but that rankles. Still, it's in a good cause. I tell him that he'll have to meet me four times that way before he can beat Stan Rutherford. You work it out in fractions."

"Don't make a nervous wreck out of Speed," the coach warned anxiously. "His over-confidence seems to have been knocked into a cocked hat, but I don't want an inferiority complex on my hands."

"He can jump eleven ten in the pole vault," said

Mickey smugly. "He did it yesterday, before my very eyes. By the time the State meet comes around, he'll either be a champion or I'll be dead." He got up stiffly and groaned. "Probably the latter."

"Mickey," said the coach warmly, "you're a pal. Why don't you run for Congress? The country needs men like you. Seriously, I'm very grateful. After all, it's for Brewster."

"A Brewster booster," said Mickey glumly. "That's me. Well, I've gotta go. Where's my hat?"

"On your head. What's the rush?"

"A little matter of two policemen coming into a room," said Mickey. "I have all my studying done, and two hours of blissful literary creation ahead. In two hours, you can write a masterpiece. Look at Shakespeare."

A voice came from the doorway. "Is Mickey here, coach?" it inquired, then broke off. "Oh, there you are, mutt. I've been turning the campus upside down looking for you."

"Hi, Glen," said Mickey.

Glen came into the room. "Er—Mickey," he said diffidently. "I wonder if you could spare me a little more time this afternoon? I've got my speech roughed out for the finals next week, and if you could—well, sort of go over it with me, sort of—well—"

"Two golden hours," said Mickey, "with two golden policemen. And now look at them!" He clapped a hand to his brow and staggered melodramatically from the room.

"Well, what's the matter with *him?*" Glen inquired with mild interest, and followed him out.

Stan Rutherford released the pole, pushing it out and away, and dropped into the jumping pit with the relaxed ease of a cat.

"Eleven foot ten," Speed whispered hollowly, clutching at Mickey for support. "I can't beat him out, Mickey, not possibly. This is his event—I never expected a first—you know I didn't. I just entered to take Bud's place. I didn't know the meet was going to depend on the pole vault. I—"

"Steady," said Mickey encouragingly. "You've done it in practice."

"Once," Speed admitted, "but it was mostly luck. Mickey, look—he can jump eleven eleven if he has to. I haven't got a chance. Oh, gosh, there goes Russ Smith out."

Russ Smith of the Blackmer squad, which was a sure thing for third place, picked himself up off the ground, glared at the bar which had clattered down beside him, grinned and shook his head.

Speed drew a deep breath. "That's not thunder," he said. "That's my knees knocking together."

Mickey patted his shoulder and pushed him forward. "Go ahead, kid," he urged. "You can do eleven ten again, since you've done it once, and maybe Rutherford can't do eleven eleven this time."

Speed picked up his pole and advanced to the mark with the expression of a martyr about to be a lion's breakfast. He ran forward with an easy springy step, and his right foot stamped down hard on the dirt as his pole struck the end of the slideway.

He soared into the air, hung for an instant parallel with the bar, then exerting violent muscular effort kicked up and over it, and, releasing the pole, dropped heavily into the jumping pit. A cheer rose from the Brewster supporters.

Mickey did an impromptu polka and flung his arms around Glen, who had wandered up. "He did it, he done it!" Mickey yelped. "He jumped eleven ten— he's crowding Rutherford. Maybe he'll get a first, and then we'll win the meet."

"Will we?" said Glen abstractedly. "Look, Mickey, you remember that part in the debate where I'm bringing up the point about the formation of the labor union system? Well, don't you think it would be better if I changed it around, so that—"

Mickey looked at him incredulously for a moment, then pulled himself together. "No, Glen," he said firmly, "leave it the way it is. You're all set, so don't go changing things at the last moment. It'll just confuse you."

"Maybe you're right," Glen began doubtfully, "only I thought perhaps— Oh, well, I guess I'm just nervous. My knees are—"

"Knocking together," Mickey finished. "Where've I heard that before?" What you need, my friend, he added to himself, is something to take your mind off your knees. "If you make any change," said Mickey, aloud, "why don't you get some more data for Stubby to use when he traces the history? There's that source book of Keene's—" After all, he told himself, Stubby won't use it anyway, and it'll keep Glen busy. "Why don't you—"

But Glen had already gone, heading for the library

like a homing pigeon, with a sublime indifference toward his school's fate in the track meet.

"Well, well," said Mickey and returned his attention to Speed, who was clamoring for it. "Swell going, Speed. Attaboy!"

Speed, however, wasn't convinced. "But that's all the higher I *can* go," he insisted. "And Rutherford's done eleven eleven lots of times."

"Once," said Mickey.

"What do you mean—once?" Speed demanded irritably. "Joe Griggs said—"

"Joe said he'd done eleven eleven in the pole vault," Mickey explained, "which was true. I told Joe to sort of emphasize Rutherford's best performance. If you get what I mean," he finished uncomfortably.

"You told *Joe?"*

"Er—yes." Mickey turned a pale pink. "You see, you were so sure that Rutherford was just a— Hmmmm. You're not mad, are you?"

"But, gee, then maybe he *can't* do eleven eleven again," said Speed dazedly.

"Maybe he can't," said Mickey.

"And maybe I *can,*" said Speed.

"Maybe you can," said Mickey.

For the fraction of a second, Speed radiated bright hope and confidence, then his shoulders drooped. "Oh, but heck—he *has* done it, and I never have."

"There has to be a first time for everything," Mickey observed sententiously.

There was, and the only person who was more surprised than Mickey was Speed. Coach Fletcher maintained an Olympic calm. He himself had anticipated eleven foot twelve and a new State record in the offing, since he was of the firm opinion that all Speed's hazards were mental.

But, compared to Glen, the coach was an emotional volcano. When Speed and Mickey shot into their room, shouting wild chants of victory and waving each other around, Glen looked up from his book, eyed them kindly, said "Hello" and returned to his book.

"WE WON!" shouted Mickey and Speed in chorus.

"You're coming to the debate with me tonight, aren't you, Mickey?" said Glen. "I'm not nervous exactly, but I like having you around. Say, you gave me a good idea about this Keene proposition. What would you think if I—"

"We won," said Speed feebly, as Mickey made a face and crossed over to Glen's side.

"Did you?" said Glen in a fatherly manner. "That's nice. Now, look, Mickey, this was my idea—"

The editor of the Brewster Daily unwound his legs from the desk and began to type a headline.

"Newton Cup Awarded Jointly," he wrote. "Speed Holloway and Glen Harris Receive Reward for Outstanding Contributions to School. State Track Title, National Debating Award—" Mickey broke off and swiveled round in his chair. "Oh. Hello."

Speed and Glen came into the room demurely, bearing between them a massive silver cup. "Ain't it purty?" said Speed, as they put it down on a convenient table and stood back to admire it.

"Swell," said Mickey sincerely. "When do you want your steak dinner?"

"Dinner?" said Glen innocently.

"Steak dinner?" said Speed. "Oh, yes—about that. Yes."

"What do you mean—yes?" Mickey inquired.

"Well, yes and no," Speed amended. "Say, Mickey, what ever became of that play you were writing?"

"Oh, that?" said Mickey. "Well, as a matter of fact, I haven't finished it yet, and the Interscholastic contest closed about a week ago, and so what with one thing and another, I—"

"How far did you get?" said Glen idly.

"Act One, Scene Two," said Mickey glibly. "Enter two policemen, carrying guns."

"Is that all?" Glen demanded. "You were that far ages ago."

"Well, yes," Mickey admitted reluctantly. "But one or two things came up, and I—"

"Such as?"

"Business matters," said Mickey. "Stop badgering me. I've gotta write a headline."

Speed picked up the cup and planted it in front of Mickey's nose. "See the pretty cup?" said Speed hopefully.

Mickey, one hand hovering over his typewriter keys, gave the engraved inscription a cursory glance. "Awarded to Glen Harris and Thomas Holloway in recognition of their outstanding contributions to Brewster Preparatory School."

Underneath was the date. Underneath the date—

"Hey!" said Mickey.

Underneath the date was a second inscription, obviously added later and in less artistic script, but perfectly legible. "Also and chiefly," read the inscription, "to Mickey Mullane, in recognition of the contest he did not enter."

"What—" Mickey began numbly.

"Well, after all, Mickey," said Speed self-consciously, "*We* ought to know why you never had time to finish your play, and—"

"Well, anyhow," said Glen. "Anyway, you know how it is. All for one, and—"

"—and two for a nickel," said Mickey, stroking the cup lovingly.

"And now," said Speed, pulling up a chair, "let *us* help *you*. What can we do to be constructive?"

"You might help me get a couple of policemen into a room," said Mickey.

FIVE CAPTAINS

CHARLIE LAWES is an enthusiast. He is also the basketball coach of Norfolk High, Stafford's most ardent rival, and therefore my arch-enemy; but the man does get ideas sometimes.

Six years ago, I was talking with Charlie and moaning because so many high school graduates never go on with their sports after graduation. Charlie agreed with me gloomily that it was too bad, and then suddenly hit me on the back with more enthusiasm than my spinal column welcomed.

"Scotty, old man," said Charlie, making another pass which I ducked, "why don't we organize a league of amateurs, each coach to use his own alumni?" Just like that it sounded good to both of us, and inside of five minutes we'd got the whole thing planned from A to Z.

The first year it was just a chance for the boys who couldn't afford to go on to college and who didn't want to give up basketball. In its third season, the idea

137

became established, and the teams are now in their sixth year, new players coming up all the time.

However, it's last year's team I'm talking about—my own, of course. To begin with, I had a bunch that would give almost any coach a thrill. At center, there was long-legged, sandy-haired "Jump" Pierce, who had captained a team of mine three years earlier and gotten All-City for two seasons. He'd been with my Amateurs for two years, as had "Red" Dayton, a forward, who had just missed All-City by a millimeter, a smooth and shifty player with a dribble that made him formidable. Red was captain when he was a junior and Jump as a senior, since I don't like anyone to have that job two years in succession.

My other forward was "Buzz" Stewart, the scrappiest player I ever knew. He captained my last team but one, jointly with Teddy King, a guard. Teddy was elected at the beginning of the season and then had to leave the team in order to work after school. The boy took it hard, and it was one of the biggest kicks I ever got out of the Amateurs to have him on a basketball team again. Both Buzz and Teddy were better-than-average players, Teddy, in fact, being certain of an All-City berth at the time he had to resign.

My other guard was a boy named Michael Crosse, who had captained my last team and was the answer to a coach's prayers. He would have made a corking center if he hadn't already qualified as a nearly perfect guard. He was fast and rangy, he could stick to his man like a shadow, and his float shot was a honey. He could dribble and pass and feint like a pro and—but you get the idea. He had the stuff and he delivered it.

I looked my Greens over with considerable enthusiasm, and even Charlie heaved an envious sigh. That season stacked up like a card sharper's deck. I couldn't see how anything less than a hurricane could keep my quint from taking everything in sight.

Before the season was over, I learned a lot.

My second team was the usual run of players, good, bad and indifferent. If they wanted to play, the purpose of the Amateurs was to see that they got a chance. Under the circumstances, it was inevitable that my first string was composed of my best bet—five captains.

And, oddly enough, I never thought to look for trouble in that quarter. The first inkling I had of what I was in for was right after our opening game, which we won, beating Tim Saunders' Blues by a nice top-heavy score. The Greens had looked good to me, with perhaps a little first-game faltering. Mike was the heaviest scorer, with Red running him a close second. I was detained after the game, so I was a bit surprised to hear voices when I reached the locker room door, and I stopped outside for a moment.

There are times when no coach should permit himself the luxury of too much conscience, and the first words I heard made me stay where I was, with absolutely no hesitation about eavesdropping.

And right here might be a good place for an explanation. I put the matter of a team captain up to the boys the first day they met, and they voted unanimously for Mike. I didn't quite like the idea of the youngest of the bunch having a captain's responsibility, but I held my tongue and waited. When I stopped outside that door, I realized I hadn't had long to wait.

"You may be captain," said a voice I recognized as Jump's, "but that doesn't mean you're the only player on the team."

Another voice—Mike's—retorted hotly. "It wasn't a question of captain or no captain," he said. "I had a chance to score, and you messed it up. What did you think I was waiting under the basket for—a telegram?"

"Steady, steady." Teddy's drawl sounded anxious and placating at the same time. "If you guys are going to start climbing all over each other, we might just as well kiss the conference cup goodbye."

Jump talked right through him, answering Mike back. "I know what you were waiting under the basket for, all right," he snapped. "A little more glory, a few more cheers—"

Teddy's voice broke in, sharply. "Mike! Don't be a darn fool!"

I guessed at trouble and opened the door. Teddy was gripping Mike's arm, and Mike was standing with his fists clenched, glaring at Jump, who was standing with *his* fists clenched, glaring at Mike. Red and Buzz were trying to pretend they weren't there, and both came to life with an innocent start when I walked in.

Talk about quick-change artists! Teddy dropped his hand from Mike's arm and patted him on the shoulder instead. Mike looked rather sheepish, and Jump took refuge in a flight of music.

"I'm just a va-a-agabond lover," he caroled, casting an anxious eye in my direction.

Teddy groaned. "Go sit on a tack," he said pleadingly. "Go put your head in a nice deep bucket of water."

"You're getting this free," Jump said without sympathy, waving a towel around in the approved grand opera fashion. "People pay good money to hear a voice like mine."

Mike chimed in, with one of his sudden reversals of temper. "If you were a radio," he said hopefully, "we could turn you off." He reached for a wet towel, poised it in his hand and looked at Jump calculatingly. "Boy, if only this was a tomato!"

Red leaped on a bench to get out of the line of fire and started yelling "Shoot! Shoot!" Mike obliged with excellent aim, catching Jump at a moment when he had his mouth open wide for another aria. When he tried to close it, it was, so to speak, full of towel.

He hauled himself out from under, flung the towel across the room and threw himself on Mike. They went down together in a chummy shower of shoes, socks and other portable objects. I decided to make an unostentatious exit and started for the door, but Mike and Jump sat up, arms wrapped around each other in what looked like a picture of brotherly love.

"Sorry, sir," said Mike, unwinding his legs from a bench and trying to get his feet under him. "Did you want us for something? This self-made crooner—"

Jump beat him gently but firmly on the head with his fists.

"No," I said. "I didn't want anything."

I escaped into the hall where I straightened my tie and my shoulders with considerable cheerfulness and assured myself that the storm had passed and there would be no more trouble in that line.

Well, we all make mistakes.

The next night when I got to practice, everything seemed to be going so smoothly that I sat down on a bench and let them do things their own way. I hadn't been there more than five minutes when I realized that their own way was not all sweetness and light.

Tommy Gray, a second stringer, neatly intercepted a pass which Jump had intended for Mike and, whirling around, he tossed the ball through the hoop. Mike took the ball off the backboard but, instead of getting back in play, he held it and stood staring at Teddy.

"I thought you were guarding Tommy," he said.

"I was." Teddy looked surprised. "He got past me."

Mike said, "He sure did, and he's not the first one to get past. You're about as much good guarding as a sieve."

Teddy stuck his hands on his hips. "Well, look who's talking," he requested. "I was a captain when you were just a scrub, Mister Wise Guy. If you hadn't been dragging your feet, you'd have got to the ball anyhow. Just because you miss a shot at the basket, so you can't show the world how wonderful you are, you get sore. You grandstander!"

"Grandstander!" Mike blew his top. "That's a sweet note. Let me tell you just one thing—somebody's got to do some scoring around here. If it was left to you, we'd be about minus ten in every game—"

"That's what *you* think," Teddy scoffed. "The great, the wonderful All-City player, Michael Crosse. I suppose I ought to feel honored to be on the same team with you. Personally," he added, "I think you're a washout. If we didn't feed the ball to you all the time, you'd be nothing at all."

"Rats!" said Jump, rather surprisingly in view of his opinions of the night before. "You know Mike's the best player, Teddy. He—"

"Oh, bunk," Teddy retorted. "He's not any better than you are. As a matter of fact—"

At this point I realized I was practically the invisible man, and I coughed as ostentatiously as possible. Both teams started and looked around at me in a stricken silence.

Mike groaned. "Holy smoke, I didn't know you were here, sir. I'm awfully sorry—"

"Go on and finish the argument," I said. "Might as well get it out of your systems."

Teddy jumped at the suggestion. "All right, then, I'll say it. I'll never get it out of my system as long as I have to be responsible to Crosse."

His using Mike's last name was a storm signal. I said, "Go on."

"That's it," Teddy said flatly. "He's too almighty high-handed." He looked to the others for confirmation, and Buzz and Red nodded their heads slowly.

Jump frowned. "I don't think that's fair to Mike," he objected. "After all, we elected him captain."

"You needn't worry," Mike said. "I resign."

Teddy groaned and kicked at a bench. "Wait a minute," he pleaded. "Don't go off half cocked. I don't mean to bust up the team or anything. I just thought maybe a different captain—I mean—" He looked at Mike and trailed off weakly.

"I didn't say I was going to leave the team," Mike said, biting the words off. "I said I resigned as captain, but I haven't the slightest intention of leaving the team. I may be a grandstander, King, but I'm not a quitter!" He snatched up a sweater and strode out of the room. The door slammed behind him, and Teddy launched another vicious kick at the bench.

"Now you really have torn it," Jump muttered.

"Quit kicking the bench, Teddy," I advised. "You'd better start electing a new captain." I waited. No comment. "You can choose someone without Mike being here," I added. "I don't think he'll mind."

"Teddy'd better be captain," Red said uncertainly.

"I will not!" Teddy nearly blew a fuse. "If I did, Mike would think I'd done it on purpose. Not that I care what he thinks," he added, a little late.

"No, of course not," I said politely, "but perhaps—"

"I say Jump," Buzz offered. "He's had most experience."

"All right with me," Teddy agreed, and Red nodded.

"Go on playing with Tommy taking Mike's place," I suggested. "I'll have a word with Mike."

I didn't though. I sat down on a bench and drew curlicues on a piece of paper, staring into space as I scribbled, and I was only faintly annoyed when I realized that the paper was my freshly typed report to the Athletic Committee.

For the next two days, things went remarkably well, and the team played such good ball that I began to

think feuds were good for the system. The day before
our game with the Scarlets, however, I noticed a
rather curious thing in my notebook. The week before
in practice games, Mike had run up fifty-one points,
an average of better than eight points a game. Since
Jump had taken his place as captain, Mike's average
had slumped to three and four points, and most of
those from free throws. An inquiry seemed to be in
order, so I asked him, in front of the others, how he
accounted for the sudden drop.

He hesitated for a moment and then glanced at
Teddy. "I didn't like to act as if—" he began, but
Teddy cut him short.

"My fault, I suppose," he offered gloomily. "Ever
since I said you grandstanded, you've been feeding
me balls so fast I get dizzy."

Jump interrupted. "I've noticed you're mighty willing to take them."

"Is that so?" said Teddy. "Well, you're not exactly
shy about grabbing your share and a little more. Any
other objections you have to my game, Your Royal
Highness?"

"Oh, shut up!" Red was kicking the paint off the
bench this time. Benches were really taking a beating
around my boys. "You make me sick, the whole lot of
you—always fighting about something." His speech
had one effect; it turned the others on him in a united
front. Mike maintained an aloof silence, and I became
aware of a severe headache.

"Suppose you play ball tonight," I said sharply,
"instead of standing around, jawing. If you don't

snap out of this, you'll take one big, beautiful licking tomorrow."

My prophecy was a hundred percent. The final score was 28 to 16 in favor of Billy Dean's Scarlets. As I left the gym, a reporter buttonholed me and asked for a statement. "Because," he said, "it's a funny thing that you can have a team like that and still lose."

"Funny!" I moaned. "Don't make me weep. I'm going home to bed— Did you ever see five mules trying to make monkeys out of each other? Well, call me up some day and I'll give you a lesson in Natural History. Good-night." I stalked off, leaving the poor guy staring after me with a strange expression.

Anyway, I wasn't much surprised the next day, when I got to practice, to find a verbal battle already well under way. Jump was beefing about the score the night before and inquiring of the world in general how he could be expected to do all the work? His remarks got stony silence from Mike and Buzz and hoot-owl laughter from Teddy and Red.

"Someone else can be captain," Jump decided suddenly. "I'm fed to the teeth."

"Even Mike would be better than you are," Teddy said.

"Thank you." Mike and Jump said it in chorus, and then glared at each other. "Suppose *you* take the job," Jump added.

"I will, just for that." Teddy stuck his jaw out. "At least, I will if it's all right with Scotty and you fellows." He turned to Buzz and Red and then suddenly observed me, standing patiently in the doorway as usual. "Oh," he said, and sat down on a bench.

I came in. "Another captain?" I inquired pleasantly. "That leaves Buzz and Red. Well, boys, don't get impatient. Around here, everything comes to him who waits. Fortunately we still have three games left—you can all have a whack at the job." They shifted uneasily and looked at the floor. I shrugged. "Well, might as well play ball. There's no sense standing around all day," I said, and blew my whistle.

You know, it's a funny thing but I never seem to learn from experience. I sat there, watching that practice, and smugly congratulated myself on having a team, at last, that really looked like something. The four boys meekly took directions from Teddy; Teddy very carefully didn't issue anything that might be mistaken for a command, and altogether it was quite pretty to watch them. The second team was swept off its feet by the wave of cooperation, and the score started to get so astronomical that I called the game off and went home, feeling quite cheerful and entertaining a charming vision of the Conference Cup.

As I said, I never seem to learn by experience. I sent my team out against Holman Craig's Whites with a light heart and it took me two quarters to realize that all was not gold that glittered.

"We'll try that play under the basket," Teddy ordered in a time-out period. "You get the ball in the back court, Red, and I'll sift through to the basket. Then you can pass downcourt to me and, if that goes for a score, maybe we can open up their defense."

Red made no answer at all, and the time out ended. Teddy, as advertised, fooled his guard and outstepped him to reach the hoop, just as Red got the ball on an interception in the back court. Teddy waited for the pass, his big paws ready to grab the ball. But Red hesitated only a second and then, completely ignoring his teammate, shot for the basket on a long spectacular try. The ball rolled maddeningly around the basket rim and fell off.

Teddy got mad and paid for it promptly by muffing a gift shot, as he was fouled. Jump made some remark I couldn't hear, and Red smiled in a rather superior fashion. Teddy called for a time out and began to bawl the whole lot of them out in no uncertain terms. Jump stared blandly at the ceiling; Red whistled cheerfully; Buzz rubbed his face with a towel, and Mike fussed carefully with a shoelace.

After a minute, Teddy gave up and asked the referee's permission to speak to me.

"Take me out of this game, will you?" he said, staring hard at the floor.

It didn't seem a good time to ask questions, but Holman Craig's boys had a three-point lead. "Get us ahead," I told him, "and I'll take you out."

I got results quicker than expected. Teddy snapped up the ball from under his guard's nose, swung around and caged a sweet long shot. A moment later, Mike dropped one in from under the basket. Teddy glanced at me, and I nodded my head and got up to look the subs over.

There was a roar from the crowd, and I turned back to see what had happened. I never did know exactly. The chief thing was that Mike was flat on his back on the floor, and Teddy was standing over him, looking wild. For one awful moment, until he spoke, I thought Teddy must have swung on Mike.

"You darned fool," said Teddy, "what do you mean barging into me, just as I was set to shoot?"

Mike got to his feet. "If you think I did that on purpose—" he began.

It was at that point that I gave up any hope of their ever getting together. I sent in the whole second team.

Throughout the rest of the game, my five captains sat in a row, studiously avoiding each other's eyes. Even when the gun ended the game, no one said a word. They might have rejoiced a little, too; my subs had gone in with the fragile encouragement of a one-point lead and had outfought the Whites, pulling the game out of the fire and winning by two points.

I followed both teams to the lockers, told the subs I was proud of them, and then took a long look at my regulars. "Well, who would you fellows like for captain now? Buzz or Red?"

Buzz kicked a cake of soap halfway across the room. "I won't be captain of this team for anybody," he announced, and Red seconded him.

"Maybe the first team had better call it a day," I suggested.

Mike said quickly, "I don't want to stop playing."

"All right," I agreed. "We'll make you captain of the sub team. No reason why you wouldn't make a good one. You made a good captain on your prep team last year. Want to try it?"

"Sure," said Mike.

"But what about me?" Red demanded indignantly. "I don't want to quit playing."

"Oh, don't you?" I tried to register astonishment. "Well, you can captain the team in the second half. I don't think those boys will mind taking orders from two captains."

"Well, but look here," Buzz began aggrievedly. "I never said—"

"Neither did I," Jump sputtered. Teddy set his jaw and kept quiet.

"Oh, all right." I thought a bit. "You can each have the team for one quarter. It'll be a break for the subs to work with first-string players. They'll be glad to get pointers from you, I guess. *They* know they're not perfect."

I got up to leave. "I guess we deserved that crack," said Mike.

Well, the idea may sound like a nightmare, but I sent the team into the game against Sam Belcher's Grays with four sub players, captained by Michael Crosse, intending to inject a first-string man each quarter.

I was completely conscious at the time and in full possession of my senses, but any reporter, coach, alumnus or student in that gym would have voted me into a lunatic asylum. With a team like mine, to send in subs!

The Grays were quite a different proposition from the team my subs had faced the week before, and we were six points in the hole before the audience had even settled down. On the sidelines, my regulars looked slightly sick.

On the floor, Mike called for time out unexpectedly.

I couldn't hear everything he was saying to the kids, but I heard enough to know it was a pep talk and I could see enough to know they were responding. They liked Mike, and he was a good player.

How really good I don't think anyone ever knew until that game. I never saw anyone put up quite that sweet a fight. He was all over the floor. His float shot was velvet; he passed and pivoted and intercepted and fought; he clung like a shadow defensively, and he burned up the court on offense. And that was all the good it did. Sam's team was "on," and, with the exception of Mike, our kids were mediocre, though the boys were game and tried like demons. The end of the quarter, in spite of everything Mike could do, found the Grays with a pretty formidable lead.

Mike walked to the bench and sat down with his head in his hands, expecting me to make the promised substitution, although by rights he should have stayed out on the floor.

Jump drew a deep breath, looking at him, and turned to me. "Why couldn't he play like that when he was playing with us?"

"He did."

Teddy glanced up. "I don't get you."

"He did play that way," I said. "So did you, so did Jump. So did Buzz and Red. The difference was that each one of you was playing against nine guys, instead of five. You were trying to beat your captain, your teammates and your opponents. Curiously enough, it doesn't make for a howling success."

"Oh," said Buzz flatly. After a minute, he said,

"Would you give us a chance—" and then he stopped, uncertain.

"You mean, would I send in my regular team?" I asked innocently.

"Yes."

"Don't see how I can," I admitted frankly. "Who'd be captain, for instance?"

"Oh, hang the captain!" Teddy exploded. "Leave Mike in. What's a captain anyhow? This is supposed to be a team."

"I'm glad you feel that way," I said very meekly. "I suppose you can go in—if Mike doesn't mind."

"I don't see why he should," Jump began hotly, and then he checked himself. "I mean, I'll ask him," he said lamely.

Somehow, Mike didn't seem to mind at all, and I sent the whole gang in just in time to keep the referee from blowing a fuse with impatience.

All my life, I've held out for the theory that a really good team can show its heels to any other team on earth if it has a real reason and the right spirit. It's always nice, I think, to have your pet theories vindicated. As the final gun went off, I gazed at the scoreboard and allowed myself a large purr. Our margin of winning was two points, but two points on the right side can be an awful lot of margin.

I was waylaid by a reporter, and, when I finally reached the locker room, I found the subs cavorting around full of beans, not at all annoyed by having been replaced so unceremoniously. The regulars, however, were busy tying shoelaces, gazing at ceilings, fiddling with towels, staring at floors, and in general doing anything except look at each other.

"Well," I said, "who's the captain now?"

"Mike," said four voices unanimously.

"Not me," said Mike.

I looked at them severely. "Don't let's start this over again," I begged. "I haven't the strength."

There was a moment's dead silence, and then all of a sudden Teddy began to laugh. He laughed so hard he nearly fell off the bench. The others stared at him for a long moment, and then, one by one, it struck them as funny too, and the howls began.

I backed out of the locker room gently. The situation seemed to be well under control, and I wanted to dream a few private dreams about next year's chances, not to mention this year's Conference Cup.

I closed the door behind me, but their whoops followed me down the hall. It takes five captains to really kick up a row like that. Or perhaps I should say one captain and four ex-captains.

At that, I still haven't got it right. Let's call it one captain plus four players—one team.

SKI HIGH

RUSTY MORRIS lay on his back and gazed somberly at his skis, which were sticking up forlornly from a large bank of snow.

"The trouble," said Rusty in a plaintive voice, "is that *I'm* still attached to 'em. Pete, do something!"

Pete Lester, who was standing by and leaning comfortably on his ski poles, shook his head. "You have to learn how to fall down and get up," Pete pointed out. "It's very important."

Rusty said he had already learned how to fall down, in fact he had learned it so well that he might just as well stay down and be done with it. Pete said he was being defeatist.

"It isn't de feet, it's de skis," said Rusty, and then rolled over hastily to get out of the way of Pete's poles which were threatening him. "All right, all right," he said a moment later, taking his face out of the snow. "I'll be good. You just tell me how to get out of this mess."

"Get your skis downhill from you," Pete advised.

"They're above your center of gravity now, the way you're lying."

"I have no center of gravity," Rusty told him sadly. "I lost it halfway down the hill, along with my balance. Boy," he added, rearing up a little to gaze at the hill he had just come down, "I sure rolled a long way."

Pete grinned slightly. "I'll admit it was a handsome spill," he said. "Come on, come on. Get your skis under you. You're going back and do that hill again."

Rusty groaned, and began to battle his way out, raising clouds of snow like a fountain. "Why I ever decided to learn to ski—" he grumbled, and then broke off, and sank back into his tunnel. "Oh, oh."

"Now what?"

"Here comes Van Parker," said Rusty. "The World's Greatest Skier—to hear him tell it. Hi, Van."

Van Parker's long legs brought him swiftly and gracefully across the powdery surface and to Rusty's side. "Did you fall?" said Van.

"Oh, no." Rusty rewarded this remark with a slightly curdled look. "I came out here to play tennis, and I just sat down to rest between sets. What do *you* think?" He turned his head slightly and noted, without surprise, that his right ski had cuddled up to his ear. "I *thought* I was feeling rather double-jointed," he murmured, pleased to have his suspicions confirmed.

"You'll never get up that way, clumsy," Van said, extending an impatient hand. "Here."

Rusty shook his head grimly. "Nope. Thanks just the same. Pete says I should learn how to fall and get up again, and by golly I'm going to. Oopf—ugh!"

Van glanced at Pete with a superior smile. "Oh,

Pete does, does he? Since when did you become a teacher, Pete?"

"Two days ago," Rusty answered for his friend. "And just now I almost came down a hill standing up—practically. I can't do a snowplow yet, but I think I've got the plot."

"You're doing very well," Pete said comfortingly.

"You should learn faster than that," Van disapproved. "Why, when I was in the Alps—"

"'Alp, 'alp," said Rusty, sinking backwards again. "Here we go on another personally conducted tour."

But Van had dropped the Alps, struck by another thought. "Suppose *I* teach you, Rusty? You'd learn much quicker and much better." He turned patronizingly to Pete. "No offense," he said. "But of course I *am* the better skier."

"Of course," said Pete dryly, "you are."

They then both looked at Rusty, who was lying flat on his back with his skis waving and his mouth making strange noises. "Well, of all the cast-iron conceit," Rusty began, loyally indignant at this insult to his friend, "you certainly take the gold-spangled chocolate bar. Why, I could learn more from Pete in a day than you could teach me in six months. And who says you're a better skier than Pete is, anyway?"

"Hush, infant," Pete soothed. "Maybe he is. Why don't you take him up, Rusty? You might learn faster, at that."

But Rusty was now quite carried away on a tide of mounting fury, somewhat hampered by his position. He had been hearing a good deal about Van's wonderful skiing the past month or more—from Van himself

—and the cool offer to replace Pete paradoxically made him boil.

"Why, in another two weeks," Rusty seethed, "Pete'll practically have me doing high jumps. You certainly have a good opinion of yourself, Mr. High-and-Mighty Parker."

Van shrugged. "Of course, if you don't *want* to learn," he said, "far be it from me to interfere. Only when I was in Switzerland, I took lessons from—"

Indignation succeeded where honest effort had failed. Rusty regained his feet at a single bound. "We've heard *all* about it," Rusty assured him, "about eighty-nine thousand times. Personally, I don't think you're so hot."

"No?" said Van idly.

"No. And what's more I'll prove it to you. Three weeks from now I'll race you down the side of Lookout, and I'll beat you, that's what I'll do."

"Rusty!" Pete wailed, suddenly realizing that he had let this argument run on too long. He was always forgetting about Rusty's red hair, which was odd as it was certainly noticeable.

Van gave a loud laugh of pure derision. "Look at what thinks it can ski!" he chortled sarcastically.

"What I can do after three weeks of Pete's teaching is something else again!" Rusty snapped. "Are you scared to take me up?"

"You aren't serious," Van told him contemptuously. "You're not even a ski-baby yet, much less a racer."

"Laugh away," Rusty invited. "Is it a bet, or are you scared you'll get licked?"

Van made a slight gesture. "If you want to be shown

up for an idiot," he murmured, "who am I to stand in your way?" He began to laugh heartily, throwing his blond head back and giving every indication of tremendous amusement.

Rusty, roused, started to express himself, but one of his skis was on an icy patch and, as he moved suddenly, it deserted him. The other stayed where it was, and Rusty, torn between them and wailing like a hoot-owl, went over backwards.

"Look who's going to beat *me*," said Van, "The World Famous Teacher and Student—what a combination!" He put his weight suddenly on his poles, sprang into the air in a graceful gelaendesprung, and coming down lightly glided away, his amused laughter floating back to them.

Rusty propped himself up with his elbows behind him and stared after Van's departing figure.

"What ever possessed you?" Pete groaned. "Of all the crazy, idiotic, dim-witted, chuckle-headed—"

"I know, I know." Rusty struggled gamely for a moment, and finally sat upright. "Only he makes me so wild—" He gave a violent shudder. "Pete, did I actually say I'd race him down the side of Lookout?"

"You did."

"Holy smoke," said Rusty, awed. "The motto of the Morrises: Talk first and think afterwards. Boy, oh boy," and he sank back into the snow.

"You said it," Pete agreed with unkind readiness.

Rusty gave a low, wondering whistle. "When will I ever learn to keep my mouth shut?" he mourned. "Pete ol' pal, something tells me we've got a busy three weeks ahead of us."

One bright afternoon, a week later, Rusty crawled out from under a large bush, where he had spontaneously come to rest, and remarked gloomily that stem-turning was his idea of first-degree insanity and that if Pete would kindly have him incarcerated, he, Rusty, would be very much obliged.

Pete brushed some snow off his friend and slapped him cheerfully on the back. "If you'd get over that trick of weighting the wrong ski," he said mildly, "you'd get along much better. Naturally, you start going in the wrong direction, and that excites you, and then you—"

"Wrap myself around the nearest bush," Rusty agreed. "Listen, I have enough trouble just coming down a hill standing up, without trying to do squeegees at the same time. Do you realize I've hardly got a whole bone left?"

"Go up and do that lifted stem turn," said Pete unsympathetically.

Rusty turned pale. "That's the nasty one where you wind yourself around your pole, isn't it? Like a blooming grapevine. I don't like that one at all, I don't."

"You'll need it coming down Lookout," Pete assured him brightly. "It's the safest and most practical way of taking very steep slopes where there are obstacles—"

Rusty swallowed hard. "Very steep? Obstacles?"

"Certainly," said Pete. "You know what Lookout's like, don't you? I mean, you've seen the trail?"

Rusty shook his head. "Just in summer. It didn't look dangerous then."

Pete clutched at his head. "No wonder you made that screwy bet with Van!" he yowled. "If you'd ever seen it— Look, Rusty, my idea is for you to take the whole trail just as carefully as you can, of course— I'm not expecting you to come in more than two hours behind Van—but, even if you take it slow—well, I mean, there *are* places where you *can't* go slow. Shambles Corner, for instance."

"Gluk," said Rusty. "*What* corner?"

"Shambles Corner," Pete said again. "It's—"

Rusty waved a feeble hand. "Don't tell me," he begged. "I can guess." He looked up at the hill he had just come down and which he had thought quite steep enough, and shook his head. "Look," he managed finally, "if you ever see me making a bet like this again, will you kindly hit me gently but firmly over the head with a hammer?"

"It'll be a pleasure," Pete told him politely. "Now, get on up there and try that lifted stem turn again."

Rusty turned and started up the hill, muttering "Shambles Corner, huh?" in a fatalistic manner. When he got high enough up for practice purposes, he turned and waved to Pete.

Pete shouted, "Pretend that patch of icy snow there is an obstacle, and make your turn just before you reach it."

Rusty nodded and shoved off.

"Skis like a poker," said Pete to himself sadly, and yelled "Relax!" in a constructive manner.

Rusty tried to obey and succeeded so well that he relaxed right down into the snow and had to start over again. This time Pete gave no advice, and Rusty arrived within striking distance of the ice patch, unweighted his inside ski and stuck his pole into the snow, intending to use it as a pivot as he had been shown.

However, as usual, he timed it wrong, stuck the pole in too soon, got it caught between his legs, tried to turn anyhow, gave an outraged squawk, and, falling backwards onto his skis, rode the rest of the way downhill in restful splendor.

"That was very pleasant," said Rusty, getting up, "and it gives me an idea. Why can't I come down Lookout that way?"

Pete gave him a long look. "I should like to see you turn those corners sitting on your skis," he said finally. "You know something?"

Rusty ignored him, still pursuing his inspiration. "I could attach a little motor and a steering wheel," he said wistfully. "Pete, must I learn that nasty lifted stem turn? It gives me the jitters."

"I think," said Pete slowly, also pursuing his own line of thought, "that it would be a very good thing for you to climb Lookout with me right now, and take a look at that trail. We won't ski—we'll walk."

When they came back, quite late, Rusty was inclined toward a thoughtful, not to say profound, silence. Finally, he drew a deep breath and said, "Which one was it that you called Suicide Curve, Pete?"

"The one with the outside bank," said Pete, feeling a certain sympathy for his pupil.

Rusty took another deep breath. "And Parachute Jump was the one that ended among the rocks that you said I'd have to miss, wasn't it?"

Pete nodded. "It's not much of a jump," he said, trying to be consoling. "Not more than six feet."

"Not more than six feet," Rusty repeated meditatively. "A mere nothing—a mere little twiddle through the air, and there you are. Look, Pete."

"Huh?"

"We never said anything in this bet about following the trail, did we? Why couldn't I come down some different way?" There was a long silence. "Aren't you listening?" Rusty demanded finally. "I said—"

"I was listening," said Pete. "Rusty, my poor fellow, I hate to break it to you, but when they cut the Lookout run they chose the easiest way of coming down, so as to make it a safe trail."

Rusty gave a gulp and shut his eyes. "Oh," he said. "How very, very cute." He was silent for a while, brooding, and then he said, "Safe trail, huh? Personally, I'd just as lief come down the side of a skyscraper."

"Ski-scraper," Pete suggested.

Rusty opened one eye and gave his friend a very pained look. "That isn't funny," he complained. "It's gruesome."

"Remember the motto of the Morrises," Pete encouraged him.

"The motto of the Morrises," said Rusty, "has been changed, by popular request. From now on, it's 'Look before you leap, and then take the elevator.' "

Word had gotten around of the stupendous skiing race to be held between Rusty Morris and Van Parker, and a considerable number of spectators stood in the snow at the bottom of Lookout and cheered impartially as Rusty and Van started the upward climb. Pete had decided to wait for Rusty at the bottom, on the perfectly sound theory that he would certainly be needed if Rusty ever arrived, and Rusty had bidden him a fond and touching farewell.

The two racers climbed Lookout in an unsociable silence, which was very hard on Rusty, because when he was nervous he was also inclined to be chatty, and on this occasion could have talked down three debating teams and a political convention with both hands tied behind him. As it was, his only comment—a dull one about the weather—elicited nothing more than a superior sort of grunt.

When they reached the top, however, Van condescended to speak.

"It's two minutes before the hour," he said, glancing at his wristwatch. "Check your watch by mine, and we'll both shove off on the hour exactly."

Rusty, whose knees were swaying in the wind, gulped and nodded.

"Sure you want to go through with this?" said Van, amusedly.

Rusty, who was perfectly sure he didn't want to do anything of the kind, drew himself up loftily. "Certainly," he said. "Why? You trying to back out?"

The only response to this effort at a retort was a short sharp laugh full of self-confidence, and Rusty looked again at his watch. The second hand moved in little nervous jerks, and Rusty felt a brotherly sympathy toward it. What he knew about nervous jerks would have filled an encyclopedia.

Van gave a shout. "See you in a couple of hours," he

jeered, and pushing off whizzed over the brow of the first hill on the run, fine snow crystals fanning out behind him.

He vanished from sight almost at once, and Rusty remembered with a hollow feeling that the first hill was more or less of a drop-off. "Oh, my!" said Rusty miserably and pushed one ski cautiously out ahead of him.

His original plan had been to close his eyes tight and shove off before he had too much time to think about it. Now, having made the initial mistake of approaching the question with his eyes wide open, he arrived at the brow of the hill with all the stately speed of a home-loving snail.

"Golly!" said Rusty, peering dismally over the edge, and backed up. Maybe there *was* an easier way down— maybe Pete was wrong—maybe . . .

He turned and went in the opposite direction in a paralyzed kind of way, with the idea of taking just one little look, but when he got to the only other possible take-off, he shuddered and turned pale.

There was a straight drop of some thirty feet, and beyond that an uninviting collection of trees. Rusty turned to leave.

What happened next was never quite clear in his mind. One moment, he was safely, if unhappily, leaving the edge of the hill. The next, the snow under his feet had crumbled and shelved, and he was flying through the air with his skis windmilling in all directions and his poles stabbing the sky in wild abandon.

Like a disorganized comet, he sped through space.

Above him was the calm summit of Lookout, which seemed suddenly a very desirable place to be. Below him was a smooth, spotless blanket of deep snow.

It was not destined to remain so long. By good luck the snow had drifted heavily under the lee of the hill, and Rusty sailed in a thoroughly disorganized manner straight into the center of a ten-foot pile, which broke his fall but effectively removed him from the landscape.

For a while there was nothing to be seen except a white expanse of snow with a large hole in it. After a while, a gloved hand appeared through the top of this hole, clutching a ski pole, and a moment later this was followed by a thatch of bright red hair.

The rest of Rusty appeared eventually like a conservative groundhog investigating rumors of sun. "Whoosh," said Rusty, making swimming motions to bring himself to the top. "Splush—foogle." He blew snow in all directions and struggled valiantly to get his skis under him again and himself on top of the snow, having a splendid opportunity to put all Pete's good advice about getting up after a fall into practice.

"Leaping hyenas!" he snorted, mastering his skis at last and beginning to dig snow out from up his sleeves and down his neck. "Some fun! What happens next?"

He gazed up at his starting place, and decided there was no getting back there again, even if he had wanted to. Then he looked below him, and gave a gratified exclamation. True, there were trees, but from here on the hill apparently dropped in a gentle, humane slope. It had been avoided for the trail, of course, he assured himself, because of the bad beginning—here he permitted himself a shudder—but from now on it looked almost navigable.

With a light heart, if a slightly shaken collection of bones, Rusty pushed off.

One of the things he hadn't yet had time to learn about skiing was how quickly an innocent-looking slope can turn into a precipice, and with what horrifying speed a skier can gain momentum once he is off to a good start.

At the beginning, Rusty had even had time to admire the scenery in a hurried sort of way. Within three short seconds, the scenery was flying by so fast that he had no way of proving there was any.

A tree popped up under his nose. He forgot everything Pete had taught him about making turns, gave a convulsive wiggle sideways and a desperate dig with his poles and felt the tree shoot past his left ear with about the hundredth part of a thin shadow to spare.

He would have yelled, but the wind of his flight stuffed the words back down his throat. He passed so close to a rock that the side of his ski screeched against it, but he was helpless to turn or stop and the hill kept on falling away from under his feet.

He had just time to think sadly of all the friends he had left behind him and to forgive Van his boasts, when another officious tree got in his way, and this time he had no chance to dig in his poles.

He sat backwards abruptly, then was thrown forward by the shock of landing and rolled head over heels down the decline like a wound-up hedgehog, with skis and poles protruding recklessly. Round and round, over and over, bump and bounce he went, until he rolled into a bush, clutched at its saving branches and pulled himself dizzily erect.

"I think," said Rusty to himself in a flat weak voice, "I'll sit this one out, thank you just the same."

The branch thought differently and divided in his hand. With a despairing shriek, Rusty felt his skis start downward again on their mad course. He went with them. He had no choice.

The drop-off this time was, as Pete would have said, "only" about six feet high, but it ended in a black-berry thicket, and the vines took a base advantage of Rusty's helpless condition on arrival and twined themselves around him and around his skis.

He got stiffly to his feet and rubbed the back of his neck, then bent down to unfasten his right ski. He had just kicked his boot loose from the binding when a rabbit shot suddenly across the track in front of him, startling him so that he loosed his hold on the ski, and it skittered down the slope ahead, basely deserting at a critical moment.

Unconsciously, Rusty made a grab for it, forgetting that he was still on a steep incline, and the movement jerked him loose and started him on a teetering, crazy, one-skied flight. It would have ended in a moment because his dragging foot slowed him, but he fell any-how and made the interesting discovery that it is pos-sible to ride a single ski as if it were an extremely nar-row sled.

Cheering weakly, he caught up with his runaway

ski at the next tree and decided forthwith to slide the rest of the way on both of them, sitting down in dignity.

"Hold it!" said Rusty to himself, suddenly valiant as he looked ahead. "That doesn't look so awful in front of me." He shook himself gently to see if any of his bones rattled, and, when nothing happened, he felt encouraged and began recklessly to strap his ski on again.

"All I want," he told himself, "is to get off this hill forever, and the quicker the better."

He gave himself a rash shove, thought better of it, too late as usual, and zoomed off down the hill.

In front of him, suddenly, was a tree. To the left of the tree was a rock. To the right of the tree was a clear open space. Rusty's mind remembered with wonderful clarity all that Pete had taught him about a stem-turn to the right. The unweighted ski swung to the . . .

You stuck your ski out to the . . .

Ah, but which ski?

"A good question," Rusty thought, and in a fleeting instant of intelligence he tried to rationalize the question in his head. Did you weight *toward* the object you wanted to miss, or away from it?

He remembered, desperately, something about an open Christiana. Surely, this was just the place for an open Christy—good, old, open Christy. He tried to get his left foot out, promptly decided it should have been his right foot, tried to get the left one back and the right one out, gave a wild hoot of utter disintegration, and finally, plunging, staggering and fighting nobly to get his skis back in some sort of relation to each other, he surrendered and dived headfirst into another of his familiar, friendly snowbanks.

This time, when he reappeared looking like Santa Claus after a hard day's work, he got a shock.

It was such a pleasant shock that it took him a moment to believe that it was true. He was at the bottom of Lookout.

He was actually at the bottom of Lookout; so far as he could tell, most of his bones were still with him; and, across the white snow, people were running toward him, waving and shouting in a frantic and irrational manner.

"Rusty! For the love of mud!" Pete had him by the collar and was hauling him out of his cozy little nest. "Say something! Are you all right?"

"No," Rusty croaked crossly. "I'm dead."

"But how'd you get here?" Pete demanded excitedly. "How'd you—"

Rusty heaved a discontented sigh, remembering something. "How many hours ago did Van get in?" he inquired morosely, putting his hand around behind his back and making a cautious experiment with his spinal column.

"Van isn't down yet," said Pete in a bewildered voice as if he suspected everyone's sanity, including his own. "I don't know what became of him." He gave his friend an exasperated shake. "How'd *you* get here?"

Rusty jerked his head toward the hill he had just come down, and then wished he hadn't. His neck seemed to be tied in knots. "Straight down there," said Rusty. "Oh, my neck! Ouch!"

"Straight—down—there?" said several wondering voices at once.

Rusty started to nod, and then decided to forego all exercise involving his neck muscles. He said "Yes" instead, and leaned heavily against Pete.

"Over the drop-off?" said Pete wonderingly. "You can't have! You're crazy."

"Are you telling me?" Rusty retorted bitterly. "However, if you don't believe me, you can go and look at my tracks. I imagine," he added thoughtfully, "they're well worth looking at. Say—" He seized Pete suddenly, forgetting his soreness. "Did you say Van wasn't down yet?"

Pete shook his head, still looking as if he had been hit on it. "No. He's vanished somewhere. I guess you've won the race, but, Rusty, I can't believe—"

"Hi," said an assured voice behind them, and Van Parker skied lightly toward the group, not seeing Rusty who was behind Pete. "What're all you fellows doing over here? I expected a welcoming committee at the foot of the trail."

"What on earth became of you?" someone demanded. "You took an awfully long time."

Van waved an airy hand and gave an amused laugh. "I waited for Rusty at the end of the first hill. Thought it'd be fun to let him get ahead and then zoom past him." He sounded aggrieved that this delightful pastime had failed to work out according to Hoyle. "In fact, I waited at quite a few different points, but he never turned up, so I finally came down anyhow." He shrugged his shoulders. "He's probably still sitting up on the top of Lookout, trying to warm his cold feet—"

At this moment, Pete moved aside, and Van saw Rusty. His mouth opened, and a strange croaking sound came forth.

After a long time, he managed something that sounded like, "Rusty! What—how—"

"Rusty," said Pete simply, "took a short-cut."

Van goggled hopelessly. "You mean, he—he—he came down *there?*"

It was Rusty's turn to wave an airy hand. "A mere nothing," said Rusty, seizing his opportunity. "An interesting little trip, but really a mere nothing."

"In three weeks!" Van was saying dimly. "You learned to ski like that in three weeks!"

"Well," said Rusty, "I had Pete for a teacher. That makes a difference." He couldn't resist the opening. "Of course," he went on solemnly, "if I'd had *you*, I could probably have learned to do that—" he gestured up at the hill, "in two weeks, or maybe even one and a half. What do you think?"

Van shook his head in awed wonder, then made a gigantic effort to recover himself. "It was a pretty good job," he admitted, "and I guess you won the race, all right. But, of course, it isn't like skiing in the Alps."

Rusty turned to him suddenly. "Tell us about the Alps," he urged enthusiastically. "We all want to hear about the Alps. *Do* tell us about the Alps."

"In the Alps—" Van began, and then Lookout caught his eye. "No. Never mind the Alps. How'd you take that first drop-off?"

"Well," said Rusty, "I'll tell you. I took it like a bird—just like a bird." He then added in an aside, for Pete's benefit only, "Just like a cuckoo."

Van registered sudden, honest admiration. "I would never have believed it possible," he said. "If you weren't actually here—"

"Skiing is believing," Rusty told him kindly. "The motto of the Morrises—revised."

RED PEPPER

"The application of literature to life!" said "Happy" Holmes bitterly, chewing at his pencil in frustrated rage. "*I* should spend the golden hours of my youth writing about literature and life." He turned for sympathy to his roommate who was lying peacefully on a sofa, and eyed him with displeasure. "Wake up, you peanut," he went on resentfully. "Talk about wasting the golden hours—look at you. Supposed to be studying Latin and all you do is snore."

"I wasn't snoring, because I wasn't asleep," said Alan Young with some dignity. "And I wasn't asleep, because I was studying Latin."

"If you're studying Latin, what are you doing on page three of the book when you're supposed to be on eighty-nine?" Happy inquired.

"I'm reviewing, since you're so curious," Alan explained hastily. "The only way to prepare for an exam is to get the work mapped out in your mind, and then—"

"I see—put the whole thing in a nutshell, so to

175

speak." Happy broke off to catch an indignantly thrown pillow, which he placed behind his head in the hope of facilitating thought. "The application of literature to life," he began again, then paused in surprise. "Are there two p's in application?"

"Huh?" Alan's head burrowed once more into the pillows.

"Oh, for the love of Mike, you asleep again?" said Happy in justifiable indignation. "I wish you'd tell me something, Alan. When you run the hundred yard dash, do you catch your naps at the fifty or the seventy-five yard marks?"

"Funny, aren't you?" said Alan.

"Screamingly, hysterically funny," Happy agreed. "How many p's did you say?"

"One—no, two." Alan took his nose out of the pillows and regarded his yellow-haired roommate thoughtfully. "There was a swell scrap in the locker room today," he remarked, "while you were out fooling with your precious javelin."

"Kindly refrain from casting aspersions on my athletic apparatus," said Happy loftily. "Who scrapped what?"

"Pepper scrapped Bobby Lee—or at least he would have if the coach hadn't come in. It was quite a go while it lasted."

"And I had to be out practicing for dear old Stannard," Happy mourned. "What the dickens is the trouble with Pepper anyhow? He's always been quick-tempered enough for any two people. How did it start?"

"I forget," Alan admitted. "Bobby tripped over a

bench and barged into Pepper, and Pepper said whyn't you look where you're going, and Bobby said why don't you get your feet out of the way, and Pepper said— well, anyhow it finished in a fight."

"A graphic and thrilling account of the battle by our star reporter will appear in the next issue," Happy murmured. "Something's got to be done about little Pepper—he's getting altogether too energetic."

"You do it," said Alan. "He has to be handled with gloves on, my little fran. You can't be too careful of the best hurdler on the whole darn team. By the way, I thought you were writing a theme on the application of—"

"Literaturetolife," said Happy hastily. "I was." He drew pencil and paper toward him again with a sigh. "Silly subject—what connection is there between Shakespeare and the track team, I ask you? Could even Julius Caesar fix things so we could beat Prescott tomorrow?"

"I doubt it," said Alan sleepily. "But I'd be willing to take a bet that you don't finish that theme this year."

"It doesn't matter," Happy conceded. "I can always square Crosby some way, if I get it in late."

"I suppose," Alan muttered, "that when you say you'll square him, you mean you'll get round him?" Two pillows landed on him suddenly, and, stuffing them under his head, he turned over and went to sleep.

Regardless of excited spectators, overworked officials, anxious marshals and shouting peanut vendors, a little group stood in the middle of Prescott field and held forth in irate argument. Two finish judges, the referee, a scorer, coaches of both teams and a track-man in Stannard blue were the chief contenders and were becoming, individually and collectively, more and more pugnacious.

"I suppose it *was* accidental," said the chief finish judge wearily, "but the fact remains that you trailed your foot alongside that fifth hurdle."

Rangy, red-headed Pepper Briscoe glared in impotent rage. "I ought to know what I did," he stated flatly. "And I know that what I didn't do was to run outside that hurdle. I—"

"I saw you," said the judge, "and so did my assistants."

"I don't care what you saw," Pepper snapped. "I didn't."

The Prescott coach put in his oar in a misguided attempt to straighten matters out, but the judge waved him aside irritably. "The decision stands," said the judge.

Stannard's mentor, "Breeze" Dalton, nodded instant corroboration. "Don't argue about it, Pepper," he said firmly. "The judges know what they're doing."

Pepper, not to be put off so lightly, flared up instantly. "The heck they know what they're doing," he sputtered. "If I'd dragged my foot around that hurdle, I'd know it, wouldn't I?"

Alan, who had joined the group, interrupted pacifically. "You might not," he said. "I went out of my lane once in a hundred yard dash, and I never knew a thing about it till afterwards."

"Unconscious as usual," put in Happy with a sigh.

"Oh, shut up," Pepper muttered. "Who cares what

you did? The point is that the judging is crazy, and—"

"Do you or do you not intend to abide by our decision?" said the judge, nodding to the referee meaningly.

"A raw deal like that?" Pepper demanded incredulously. "I most certainly do not."

"All right then." The referee took his cue. "Get off the field." Coach Dalton groaned inwardly, but acquiesced immediately to the order.

"But I can't," Pepper protested. "I'm running in the two-twenty hurdles too." He looked about him for confirmation.

"Oh no, you're not." The referee was polite but firm. "You're disqualified from this meet for refusing to obey official instructions. Now clear out before I decide to send in a statement to the registration committee."

Pepper showed signs of being more than willing to go on with the argument in his own way, and it took the combined efforts of Happy and Alan to remove him from the scene of battle. Safely arrived at the locker room, they undertook simultaneously and unwisely to lecture Pepper on his shortcomings, but their well-meant efforts were met first with a lowering silence and then with snorts of pure derision.

"Look at Happy!" Alan exhorted. "He was disqualified in the Huntington meet because he stepped on the board, but did he bite the judge's ear off? He did not. He—"

"Little Rollo," said Pepper witheringly. "Anyhow he *did* step on the board, and the point is that I *didn't* go outside the hurdle, and no cockeyed judge can—"

"Tsk, tsk," said Happy.

"It's all very well for you to be so funny," Pepper went on in frantic exasperation. "You always have things easy anyhow—"

"I? I have things easy?" Happy clutched his hair in unbelieving horror. "Me with a term theme due on literchoor and life, me with the dates of the Punic Wars to learn, me with—"

"Oh, will you shut up?" Pepper sprang to his feet in a burst of rage and gave Happy a hard push which knocked that youth against a bench, over which he promptly fell, landing on the floor with his feet in the air and astonishment written large on his countenance. Pepper glanced at this pitiful spectacle coldly and strode from the room, slamming the door behind him so energetically that three hats fell off their hooks.

Alan and Happy regarded each other in a long silence, during which Happy's feet continued to wave feebly. Then their owner spoke. "This," he said, "is a bit thick."

Alan nodded.

"In fact," Happy pursued the subject, "I might go so far as to say that it's a bit too much. Could you possibly in the kindness of your heart move an inch or two to the right and haul me out of here, or would that be too great a strain? Thank you."

He got to his feet and dusted himself off sadly, then sat down on the bench and frowned, elbows on knees and chin on hands.

Alan stood the unnatural silence as long as he could, then burst out. "If Pepper only—"

Happy raised a warning hand. "Shhh," he commanded. "I'm thinking."

Alan regarded him with grave pity. "Poor chap, you've got yourself mixed up with someone else, that's what it is. That fall must have done you more harm than I thought."

"Will you shut up?" Happy requested plaintively. "I've got an idea."

"What!?!"

"Don't be so funny," said Happy with a pained expression. "I mean to say—Shakespeare."

"Milton," Alan supplemented promptly.

Happy again clutched his brow. "*Now* what are you talking about?"

"Sorry," said Alan. "I thought we were playing a game." He waited patiently for further explanations.

"Shakespeare," said Happy, "and are you going out tonight because, if you are, don't. Now tell me, are you?"

"Certainly I'm going out," Alan rejoined indignantly. "I'm dining with the Shah of Persia and the Sultan of Egypt, or wherever they have sultans. What did you think I was doing?" He gave Happy a long look full of woe. "Listen, for the love of Pete—what's come over you? Why all this mystery?"

"*You* listen," said Happy feverishly, starting for the door. "Stick around here and get about five of the fellows on the team to come over to our diggings tonight. See?"

"But why?" wailed Alan.

Happy turned, his hand on the doorknob, and regarded Alan thoughtfully. "To discuss things," he said darkly. "Specifically, my good fellow, to discuss life and literature. Even more specifically, 'The Taming of the Shrew.' And by the way," he added, "don't invite Pepper."

Bobby Lee, high jumper, took his nose out of his locker and surveyed the assembled team placidly. "And if we win the tri-school meet next week, we'll be sitting on top of the world. The honor of Stannard therefore depends on whether I get fourth or fifth place for my charming and delightful version of the Western roll."

"This team as a whole talks too much," said Happy pensively.

"That comes well from you, I must say," Alan remarked. "You talk more than any other person in the world, without exception."

"Alan, you forget yourself," said Happy sweetly. "Say, Pepper, toss me that shoe, will you?"

Pepper, who was struggling madly with a buckle, glanced around. "What shoe?"

"The one behind you," said Happy, pointing.

"It's as near to you as it is to me," said Pepper. "Run your own errands."

Happy raised his eyebrows but got up silently and retrieved the shoe for himself, taking the opportunity at the same time to remove one of Pepper's from the bench. He then sat down with a gentle smile and awaited developments. Pepper felt around for his shoe, failed to find it and then noticed it between Alan and Happy. He started to speak, then checked himself, and glared at Happy who was whistling Yankee Doodle with variations. "Pass me my shoe, will you, Alan?" said Pepper.

"It's as near to you as it is to me," said Alan mendaciously. "Run your own errands."

Pepper flushed. "Being funny, I suppose?"

"Some say yes and some say no," Alan admitted lightly. "Some misguided people don't appreciate my peculiar brand of humor. In a way, I suppose I *am* being funny, but I'm not going to pass you your shoe. Come and get it—you need the exercise."

Pepper reluctantly got up and came over. "A swell bunch of guys you are. All I do is ask a little favor, and you act as if I'd killed you. The whole shooting-match of you make me sick—never do anything but quarrel." He put on his shoe, snatched up his collar and tie and started for the door.

Ted Harris crossed his legs and leant back luxuriously against the wall, his feet sticking out in the aisle. Pepper, paying no attention to where he was going, promptly fell over them and landed sprawling on the floor. Before he could collect his wits enough to express himself, Ted exploded in intense wrath.

"Can't you look where you're going, you big ox?" he snapped. "The whole floor to walk on and you have to fall over my feet. I suppose if I climbed up on the ceiling, you'd trip over my ears. Great guns, Pepper, do you think you own the whole darn locker room?" He paused for breath, but the sight of Happy silently applauding behind Pepper's back urged him on. "Wouldn't you like this bench too, while I think of it?" he continued with heavy sarcasm, "and all the field outside, too, to flop over, and I'll go to Asia where I can wear my feet without having dumbbells like you tramping all over them."

At this piece of injustice, Pepper got up dazedly and regarded Ted in open-mouthed incredulity. Then, unable to find any words to express himself, he walked toward the door and let himself out, his collar and tie left lying neglected on the floor.

As the door closed behind Stannard's star hurdler, Ted heaved a deep sigh and patted himself affectionately on the back. "Am I good," he chortled, "or am I good? Mr. Barrymore in person, that's me."

"It's working," said Happy complacently. "It may take a little time, but with a heavy dose of the same at frequent intervals, we'll have Pepper yet so that he'll behave like a human being instead of a bear."

"We're to keep up the good work then?" said Alan.

"Sure," said Happy. "Every time he starts to blow up, you blow up a little harder and a little faster. But for the love of lemons, fellows," he added, suddenly struck by a thought, "don't get the poor kid so upset that he can't run a decent hurdle race. Breeze is counting plenty on what he'll do in the 120 and the 220. Those are the most doubtful races in the whole meet, with Thurman from Lee and Dexter from Hillman both so good. And we need them points, gentlemen, we need them points."

"You going to get a first with your little javelin, Happy?" said Stub, looking in dismay at a pile of tangled shoelaces.

Happy groaned. "The chances of my beating that

Hillman fellow are about as good as the chances of my climbing the Matterhorn next week. I'll get a second maybe, if I'm a good boy and Santa Claus likes me."

A week later, the Stannard locker room was a scene of bedlam with the tri-school meet about to start. Frantic and unreasonable demands flew through the air, and life for the unhappy manager, Stub Thompson, was nearly unbearable.

Stub climbed onto a bench to remove a jersey from the top of a locker and stepped off heavily onto Pepper's foot. "Oh, sorry," he apologized.

Pepper eyed him morosely and started to speak, but checked himself. " 'Sall right," he said gloomily.

Alan nudged Happy. "It *is* working," he whispered jubilantly. "Less than a week of treatment, and the patient is practically as good as new."

The clerk of the course stuck his nose around the door. "Heats for the hundred, 120 hurdles and mile run," he intoned. "Get going; the meet starts in five minutes."

Happy dashed across the field and seized Alan enthusiastically. "Good man," he said, "I knew you'd get a first."

"Uh-huh," said Alan. "I remember. You had it all figured out."

"We've qualified two men for both low and high hurdles," Happy crooned. "Thurman and Dexter are in, of course, and Pepper, and so's Buzz. And someone says that Tommy Hollister looks like a sure thing for the pole vault, so we might be able to do something about this meet after all, if everything goes our way."

"Well, if it doesn't," said Alan, "you can comfort yourself with the thought that you hit the bullseye with Pepper. Boy, when he apologized to Stub, I nearly fainted away."

"You and me both," Happy confessed. "What say we watch the low hurdles?"

"Finals for the low hurdles—220," the starter echoed him. The runners stepped eagerly to their places, and the starter raised his gun. "On your marks! Get set!" The pistol cracked, and the runners flew off from their marks. The gun went off again, and the men halted in their tracks like frightened rabbits. The starter motioned them back to their places with a jerk of his head.

"False start, Briscoe of Stannard." He waved a hand at Pepper. "Watch out," he advised kindly. "Another one of those would disqualify you."

"If that was a false start," said Pepper grimly, "I'm a Dutchman."

"Can't say what country you're from," said the starter, "but a false start it was. And another one will make two, and two will disqualify you, and will you kindly get into place and not keep everyone waiting?"

"If you think I beat the gun deliberately," Pepper began, hands on hips and jaw out-thrust.

"Who said anything about beating the gun deliberately?" said the starter peevishly. "I said you made a false start. There are about seven hundred different ways of making a false start, and yours was one of them. Now *will* you get back into place, or shall I disqualify you here and now?"

Fifty yards away, Happy clutched Alan's arm. "I

never thought of this," he wailed. "We reformed the guy for team purposes, but I forgot all about what he might do when he got out on the field. Of course he wouldn't lose his temper with us when we ganged up on him, but like an imbecile I never thought of what he might say to an official. Shades of Shakespeare, if I can only beat him to the draw!"

"Well, do *something!*" said Alan.

"I will," Happy promised, starting off at a run. "Bang, bang, the British are coming. Lafayette, we are here." He skittered to a stop, practically under the starter's nose.

The starter, thoroughly out of patience and about to send Pepper from the field, looked upon Happy with something approaching madness. "What are you doing here?"

Happy threw discretion to the winds. "Of all the rotten officiating, that takes the cake," he said at the top of his voice. "What do you think you're here for? Why don't you stay home and make mud pies? That's all you're good for. False start, my eyebrow! You don't give your orders right, that's all. You—"

"Happy!" said Pepper.

"Happy!" said Coach Dalton, appearing from the sidelines.

Happy drew another deep breath, and appealed to the world in general. "He—" his finger pointed accusingly at the outraged starter—"can't start a race right, and the poor fish thinks he can. He gets everything wrong and then blows up when someone tells him so. And furthermore and likewise—"

"Are you a Stannard team member?" the referee interrupted calmly.

"Yes, I am, and what's more—"

"Then get off the field and don't come back, and be grateful I don't do anything more about it. Of all the unwarranted impudence—"

"But he's in the javelin event," said Pepper bewilderedly.

"Not today he isn't," said the official. "Now go ahead with the race."

The starter, having forgotten how the argument began, signaled the runners to their places. Pepper made a frantic grab at Happy, but that young man shoved him into place and hissed in his ear, "Don't be a sap. I couldn't have gotten more than a second place anyhow. Get going."

The starter suddenly bethought himself of Pepper's delinquencies. "Now remember, another false start and you're automatically disqualified," he warned.

"Yes, sir," said Pepper meekly.

At the crack of the gun, Pepper got off to a clean start and hit the first hurdle in perfect stride, keeping low and concentrating on the bar ahead. Thurman was half a stride slow, and Dexter was late in getting down to the ground. Pepper took the second hurdle ahead of the field, amid frantic partisan cheers. Well trained in racing, he kept his eyes fixed determinedly on nothing but the next hurdle as he cleared one after another, never once trying to check his position. The last three hurdles swam into his line of vision—the most dangerous in the race, when a man is both fatigued and excited. Dexter knocked one over and lost a step. Buzz stumbled and fell, jumping to his feet instantly, but out of position for placing.

Thurman stuck grimly with Pepper, and they went over the last hurdle, shoulder to shoulder. Pepper clenched his fists, rose high on his toes, and sprinted for the tape, flinging himself forward in a spectacular finish and streaking over the line, a fraction of an inch in the lead.

"And then in the second hurdle race, Dexter knocked over the next to the last one and went off his stride— he was tired anyhow—and Pepper just breezed in. Gee, it's too bad that you missed it." Stub finished his exposition in a breathless rush and patted Happy's shoulder sympathetically.

"Here comes the team," said Happy, as a torrent of noise swept over the outside hall. The door burst open, and runners, jumpers and weight men poured into the room, stumbling over each other in their haste.

"Yeaaa!" Buzz shouted. "Did we take 'em or did we take 'em?"

"We took 'em," said Alan more temperately, and sank on a bench to gasp.

"Where's Pepper?" said Happy.

"Coming. The coach wanted to give him a few medals or something. Boy, oh boy, what a race *he* ran. Whe-ew." Buzz sank back into Alan's arms, overcome by the memory. The door opened slowly. "Here he is," said Buzz.

Pepper walked into the room and planted himself

in front of Happy. "Thanks for the rescue," he said coldly. "I'm sorry you had to be disqualified."

"Quite all right," said Happy, not too comfortable and feeling that there was more to come.

"I suppose," Pepper went on relentlessly, "that you're back of all this that's been going on this week?"

"All what?" said Happy, too innocently.

"Making a fool of me," said Pepper hotly. "Picking fights, just to show me up. A put-up job, wasn't it? Go on, why don't you? Answer me." He towered over Happy who was practically falling off the bench.

Happy opened his mouth. "It was this way, Pepper," he said placatingly. "You kept losing your temper, see?" He waved his hands expressively. "And you kept stirring things up on the team, see? And you got into a fight in the Prescott meet and everything, and something just had to be done. So—"

"Go on," said Pepper.

"Well, give me a chance to explain, will you?" Happy's voice was plaintive. "I had this theme, and it was supposed to be about the application of literature to life— Don't look like that; it's really quite simple. And I got to thinking about Shakespeare and I got to thinking about you, and then I put two and two together—"

"Talk sense," Pepper commanded.

"Oh gosh," said Happy desperately, "didn't you ever read 'The Taming of the Shrew' by a guy named Shakespeare?"

Pepper's fists clenched, his eyes snapped, and he swung on Happy. "So that was it? That was what—"

He got no further, but collapsed on the nearest bench, suddenly, like a pricked balloon, his mouth opening and closing like a fish's.

Happy stared at him, unable to believe his senses. Unquestionably and incredibly, Pepper was laughing. Each fresh paroxysm of mirth shook him so that he nearly fell off the bench, and the tears streamed down his cheeks.

"Well, for Pete's sake," said Stub, "tell *us* the joke."

Pepper mopped his eyes and gasped for breath. "I couldn't go on with it," he gurgled. "It was Happy's face. Did you ever see anything like it in your life?"

"Undoubtedly not," said Alan gravely, "but what's the connection? What *is* this anyhow?"

"He thought I was serious," Pepper moaned. "You all did, you asses. Well, it just shows what I always suspected—I ought to be on the stage."

"Do you mean to say," said Alan, "that all this scene was just an act? But what—how—"

"You idiots," said Pepper affectionately, "how long do you think it takes a guy to get hep to himself? Heck, I *thought* I knew what you were up to yesterday, but great snakes! when Happy got himself thrown out of the meet just because I behaved like a darn fool —well, I can take a hint."

"And all this song and dance?" said Happy feebly.

Pepper grinned. "I had to even things up, didn't I? And besides, you might have forgotten what a real temper was like, unless I gave you something to remember mine by."

"Well, I'll be a tut-tut-tut," said Happy. "Stymied, checkmated and buncoed. Me and Shakespeare collaborate, and then the actor gets all the bouquets. There ain't no justice. Come along, Alan. I won't be able to walk away under my own power."

"Where you going?" said Alan, reluctant to leave.

"Home," said Happy laconically. "Haven't you heard? I've got an English theme to write."

"Another one?" said Alan with a heartfelt groan.

"Well, not exactly," said Happy. "This one is about literature and—er—life."

"The same literature and the same life?" said Alan politely, with a wan smile.

Happy nodded sadly. "Yes, the same theme, so to speak. It's late, I admit, but after all—" he paused and looked around the room. "After all," he finished triumphantly, "look at the research work I've been doing."

ALIAS ALL-AMERICAN

"WITH my ba-hanjo on my knee!" The singer finished with a warble and a bow.

"The difference between you and a calliope, Ted," said Nicholas Rand unkindly, "is that a calliope has some trade-in value."

"The beauty of my voice," said Ted Benedict with reproachful dignity, "is quite impervious to your nasty insinuations. As a matter of fact—hey! Those are *my* shoes."

"I know it," said Nick calmly. "Nice fit, aren't they?"

"Gentlemen," Ted said tragically, addressing the crowded locker room, "I demand justice. That mug who calls himself a football player has burglarized my dearest possessions. Am I to cavort for dear old State in these dilapidated wrecks?" He held up Nick's shoes. "These tottering apologies for footwear? These—"

"Shut up, my little man," said Bill Baker, captain and center of the State College eleven, soothingly. "And sit down." He turned sternly to Nick, who was unrepentantly tying a shoelace. "Prisoner at the bar, as a lowly member of the scrubs—"

"Not lowly," said Nick reprovingly.

"Well, a member of the lowly scrubs, then," Bill obliged.

"Hey!" said the entire scrub team, looking dangerous.

"Blast," remarked the self-appointed judge. "All right, all right. Anyway, what have you to say in your defense?"

Nick rose and bowed. "Sir, he said in manly tones," said Nick, "I can only say that I am not myself today." He observed the light of repartee in Ted's eyes, and continued hastily. "Today I am the great Jim Winters of Gregg University, who will honor us with his presence next Saturday. Gentlemen, I demand the rights of an All-American halfback."

"Case dismissed," said Bill humbly, "and defendant may keep the shoes." He dropped the pontifical tone. "So you're alias All-American again, huh? That's your second this year—we're moving in lofty circles."

He referred to the custom of having one player on the scrub team represent the star of the opposition, in practice. Nick, as the best player on the scrubs, frequently doubled for the mighty, and the 53 on his jersey today was well known to fans who had watched the meteoric Winters blaze a trail across the football horizon. The State scrubs had devoted several days to certain Gregg plays starring Winters, while the varsity studied methods of defense. State, with no outstanding star, boasted a strong line, brilliant teamwork and a speedy backfield. Bill Baker at center, Ted at guard, and a flaming-haired quarterback named Red Mehaffey were candidates for All-Conference honors, and the

team was still undefeated in its fourth week of competition. The war-cry of the hour was "Stop Winters!"
and the State coaches were bending every effort to
this end.

Twenty minutes after Nick's acquittal, head coach
Blaine, a stocky man of middle years, called the squad
together. "Okay. You know this double reverse thoroughly, and you can stop it on paper. Let's see if you
can on the field." He put a hand on Nick's arm. "This
is Jim Winters, number 53. If you stop him on this
play, you stop the play. *Get him.*"

"Nice send-off," Nick muttered. "Just like an early
Christian martyr being fed to the lions." He joined the
scrubs at midfield and pulled his helmet on cheerfully.
"Wait with this play, Tom," he told the quarterback.
"Lure them on with a couple of simple combinations,
and then we can mow 'em down."

Tom Nelson all but purred in anticipation, as the
teams lined up pugnaciously. Two line plunges were
smothered, but on third down the varsity got edgy
and drew an offside penalty. Tom played this advantage and signaled for the reverse from a formation
strong to the left. Tubby Green at full took the ball,
pivoted and faked a pass to Dick Simmons, then spun
all the way around and shoved the ball into Nick's
hands, whereupon that temporary All-American went
off the weak side in a reverse.

The play worked almost too well, and Nick shot
through a baffled varsity line for twenty yards, before
the secondary ganged up on him. Coach Blaine wailed
loudly, while the varsity blushed and the vainglorious

scrub team puffed out its collective chest and crowed.

"I sit up nights to plan a defense," said Blaine, enlarging his grievance, "and then you do *that*. What became of you fellows? Bill, you were all right, so was Ted. But you two—" He turned indignantly on Slim Edwards at end and Joe Page at tackle. "What became of you?"

"They fell into a transom," Nick quoted sadly, and the coach grinned in spite of himself.

"A couple of transoms," he agreed, his wrath cooling. "Okay. We'll walk through the play as many times as necessary, *until you can stop it*. You know your assignments. *Do them.*"

The team lined up again and walked slowly through the play, accompanied by a running fire of comment from Blaine. "Watch Winters," he cautioned, mopping his brow. "Go through it again—slow, slow. Here comes Winters. *Watch him.*"

Nick grinned and jogged peacefully along, wishing for the moment that he really were Winters—Winters in fast motion, streaking toward the enemy goal. Might be nice to be All-American, instead of a second-year scrub masquerading as a football hero. In prep school, Nick had shown promise; as a frosh, he had also shown promise. He was still showing it, and still on the scrubs. There were times, like that run just now, when Nick felt confusedly that he should be good enough for a varsity post. Coach Blaine occasionally thought so too, but the present varsity left half, Douglas Lee, was a first-class man, and his running mate, Skid Prentiss, was steady and dependable. The coach thought for the hundredth time that Nick's weakness could be summed up perfectly in the phrase, "He doesn't play football; he plays at it."

"Have you got it now?" said the coach, dismissing Nick's future with a sigh.

Slim and Joe, feeling themselves chief offenders, nodded eagerly, and the coach smiled. "The thing looks different on paper," he said forgivingly. "O-kay. We'll take it fast now, and this time *get* Winters."

Tom called an end-run and an off-tackle slant before he gave Nick his signal. This time the play was wholeheartedly smothered, and Coach Blaine smiled his satisfaction, while the scrubs in a glow of sacrifice rubbed their bruises thoughtfully.

An hour later, Ted and Nick left the athletic building and headed across campus for their room.

"Got much studying to do, Nick?" Ted inquired casually.

"Nope," said Nick, "except that economics outline. Why?"

"Oh, nothing."

They walked on in silence, then Ted spoke again. "As a matter of fact, I feel chatty. Sit down a minute, and lend me your ear."

Nick flopped unceremoniously onto a convenient pile of leaves, Ted beside him. A long and weighty silence ensued, broken impatiently by Nick.

"I thought you felt chatty," he complained. "Compared to you, an oyster's an after-dinner speaker." He glanced curiously at his companion. "Something on your mind, Ted?"

"You are," said Ted.

"Me?" Nick registered elaborate horror and clutched his brow.

"Cut the comedy," said Ted. "I mean it."

"Go on," Nick suggested soberly.

Ted hesitated a moment, then blurted out his speech without ornament of tact. "Look here, Nick," he said, "where does all this fooling around on the scrub team get you? Why in blazes don't you get busy and get a regular berth? At least, play good enough football to get into more games, so you'll be varsity next year."

Nick's eyebrows, which had shot up at the beginning of this tirade, came slowly down to normal. "The coach doesn't appreciate my peculiar style of playing," he said with mock sadness. "What's hit you, Ted? Talk sense. I'm just not good enough for the varsity."

"You make me tired," said Ted, so intensely that Nick stared. "You could be a swell player, and instead you just fool around, playing Jim Winters this week and someone else next week. Every so often you pull out some real football like this afternoon—"

"That was the play," Nick interrupted.

"The play, my hat!" Ted exploded. "We knew how to stop it—you just came through too fast. Blaine knows that, even if he did lambast Joe and Slim. You could have pulled it again, but as soon as you thought you ought to be stopped, you *were* stopped."

Nick chuckled. "You flatter me, suh," he murmured, dropping an arm affectionately across his friend's shoulders. "You've got a lot of beautiful illusions about me, Ted. I'm no future All-American. If I played better football than Doug and Skid, I'd be on the varsity. But I can't, and so I ain't."

"You could if you'd try," Ted insisted stubbornly.

Nick laughed lightly. "Delusions of grandeur. I'm much obliged for your overwhelming opinion of my talents, but I'm afraid it's all a beautiful dream. What the heck, Ted? I have fun."

"Yeah, you have fun and so you—" Ted broke off and finished with a barely audible "quit." Nick elected to misunderstand the word.

The following Saturday, State College took a sluggish Gregg team to town and effectively bottled up the prized All-American half, who if the truth were known was suffering from an off day. Joy reigned at State over the one-point victory, and predictions for a conference title were heard on all sides.

But that evening the peace of Fairchild Hall was shattered by a modern Paul Revere in the person of Red Mehaffey, who burst in on Ted and Nick as they wrestled with Parliamentary Law.

Red flopped informally on the nearest bed, paused for a moment and dropped his bombshell. "Hear about Skid Prentiss?"

Nick dropped his pencil, dived under the table and bumped his head coming up. "What about Skid?" he inquired, rubbing the injury peevishly.

"Strained his ankle," said Red laconically, producing an apple and chewing enthusiastically.

"What do you mean—strained his ankle?" Ted demanded. "I saw him an hour ago, and he was all right then."

"Ah, but that was then," said Red brightly. "He fell down the Auditorium steps. Doc says it's a minor sprain, but he's out of the Center game."

"Gee, what rotten luck," said Nick sympathetically. "I suppose Bob Cross gets his place?"

"Use your brains, laddie," Red suggested. "Bob hasn't worked off that condition in Psych yet. He can't play."

"Gosh, that's right. Then who—Steve Harris?"

Red grinned widely. "Nope. You, my modest little artichoke, you. The coach said, said he, that Center being only a breather, you couldn't do *much* harm although he feared the worst, and—"

Nick looked around for something to throw, and Red moved energetically toward the door. "Well, I must be off."

"You are," Nick agreed, "but I didn't think you knew it."

"Bah to your insults," said Red haughtily. "Well, I shall expect big things of you next Saturday, my own, my beautiful teammate-to-be. If I had some liquid, I'd drink a toast—may you gallop to glory and whatnot."

"Toast isn't a liquid," Nick objected practically. "It's a mineral, and you burn it. If you're going to drink my health, you need something wet."

"Oh well, buttered toast then." Red bowed himself out to inaudible cheers, and Ted turned eagerly to Nick.

"Here's your chance, Nick," he exulted.

"Oh, sure," said Nick with heavy sarcasm. "One breather game, with Skid probably back next week, and right away you make me the player of the century."

"Well, it *is* a swell chance."

"Sure. Only I have a better one of flunking this

quiz tomorrow. Here." He picked up the discarded
book. "What do *you* know about parliamentary law?
Neither do I."

Ted however was lost in thought, and Nick joggled
his elbow firmly before he could get a response. "What
do you care what I do in the line of dying for dear old
State?" he asked curiously. "Why this passionate desire to do me good?"

"Don't ask me," said Ted wearily. "I guess I'm
screwy. But I still think you could go places Saturday."

He was due for a rude awakening. State breezed
through on the long end of a 32 to 7 score, but Nick's
part in the victory was minor. The envisioned gallops
to glory failed utterly to materialize, and none of the
spectators had occasion to check his number.

The usually calm and self-contained Ted released a
flood of pent-up indignation in the locker room after
most of the squad had gone, with only Bill, Red and
Nick as witness to the unexpected performance.

"You know darn well you quit," Ted seethed. "You
practically *walked* through the plays—"

"I did my job all right, didn't I?" said Nick coldly.

"That's all you did do," Ted sputtered angrily. "You
went through the motions, and there it ended. Get
wise to yourself, Nick! You can play football." He appealed to Red and Bill, who nodded agreement. "Only
you never try. You've got into a habit of being alias
All-American, and you depend on the play to see you
through, instead of on yourself. Great scott, man, football games aren't won on the plays. It's what the team
does with the plays."

"Continued in our next," said Nick wearily. "Calm down, Ted. It's only a game."

"It's a game all right," Ted admitted, "but it isn't *only* a game. And, even if it is, you don't have to—quit."

Nick's voice was like an icy shower. "I suggest you cut that word out of your vocabulary where I'm concerned, Ted," he said, and snatching up a sweater he strode out of the room.

With Skid back in the lineup, State pointed definitely for the final game against University, on which the conference title depended. With Chuck Davis, University's candidate for All-American, going great guns for the Big Green, there was ample cause for worry in the State camp. Coach Blaine scouted University and spent days preparing the varsity, while the scrubs followed their usual procedure and Nick got heavy workouts in an alias-Chuck Davis role. As the varsity caught on, he was effectively smothered, and Coach Blaine wore a beam which spread from ear to ear.

At this juncture of State history, Ted succumbed and decided to do something about his difficult teammate. The system was simple. Three of University's most effective plays were over defensive right guard, Ted's own position. So effective were these in fact that Davis was accustomed to ripping off considerable yardage on them, and Coach Blaine had been much exercised to plan an adequate defense. Only one of these plays had been tried so far this afternoon, and then only experimentally.

Now, with this same play coming up again, Ted obeyed impulse and decided to let himself be taken out so that Nick would look good. He did this so effectively that Nick shot through in a rather startled fashion for fourteen yards.

"Defensive right guard," shouted the coach wrathfully. "What are you doing?"

"Sorry, sir," said Ted meekly, and on the next play got through to the runner but muffed the tackle. Practically speechless, Coach Blaine strode in among the players and signaled Ted out for attention.

"What are you up to, Benedict?" he inquired. "You know your assignment. Davis will make a Roman holiday out of you, if you play like that Saturday."

"I know, sir. I'm sorry." Ted's face was a study in contrition. "Only—it's funny—even when I got to Nick, I couldn't stop him. Something in the way he runs."

Blaine planted his fists on his hips, and studied the guard suspiciously, then glanced over at Nick who was looking baffled. "Let's have it again," said the coach meditatively.

They had it again, and this time Nick, with a vague feeling that Ted was getting into hot water, saved his roommate any necessity of making him look good, and to Ted's surprise and pleasure flashed through for considerable yardage again. Coach Blaine scratched his head, then signed to a substitute guard.

"You're not looking too good in there, Ted," he said, "and it's just a little hard to believe that it's all Nick's running or a scrub's blocking. Your playing's been a bit—preoccupied lately. Getting a little stale?"

Ted looked startled. "I—no, sir."

"Might be," said the coach reflectively. "Maybe we should bench you for a few days. Or is there something on your mind?"

"I—no, sir."

The coach's frown deepened. "Well, we'll let someone else have a whack at Nick and, if he can't stop the play, we'll take it as read and figure out a better defense. Otherwise, I think you'd better have a few days off, Ted. Okay, let's go."

Nick's puzzled thoughts caught him up abruptly. If he got through this time and spoiled the defense, it would satisfy the coach that Ted wasn't at fault.

Nick eyed the substitute guard apprehensively—a very large and solid guy, he thought. Offense was going to have a sweet time blocking him out, and the play went right over him. If he didn't block and stay blocked, Nick was going to be caught in a large way. Unless he was faster than an express train and slipperier than a greased pole. Swell chance. Well, he could always *try*.

Defensive guard was not blocked out of the play, owing to his fanatical determination to be in the thick of things, but nevertheless it was a much annoyed linesman who tackled thin air and saw Nick sneak past for a twenty-yard gain.

The varsity was furious and said so in no uncertain terms. Ted tried not to look stunned, and Nick registered nonchalance. The coach scratched his nose and said, "Hmmm." Then he turned to Skid Prentiss and asked after the injured ankle. Skid said with false heartiness that it wasn't so bad, and the coach said "Hmmm" again and sent him to the showers.

"Nick," said Coach Blaine, "take Skid's place on the varsity for a while. You didn't look bad in there. We'll see how Ted gets along with you behind him."

Behind a varsity line, Nick had himself a field day. With the incentive of his desire to make Ted look good, he coaxed a bewildered Red to send him repeatedly over his own guard—a system which raised havoc with the scrubs and gave Ted a surplus of exercise.

When the squad trotted off the field, Coach Blaine signaled Ted to his side. "Nick didn't look bad," the coach said. "Pleases you, doesn't it?"

Ted admitted it did. "Why not give him a chance Saturday?" he urged. "He's better than Skid really when he gets going."

"When he gets going, yes," said the coach dryly. "Only how many times a year does he really try like today? No, I can't depend on him, Ted. Game's too important. Might use him as a spot runner though."

"I think he'd make good if he had a chance," Ted insisted.

"Nick's had nothing but chances," said the coach. "He likes football and he's a natural player, but he fools around and enjoys himself, and that's all. No, I can count on Steve Harris to replace Skid better if it's necessary. Might use Nick as a spot runner though—probably will. You can tell him that."

"I will," said Ted, and started for the showers.

"Hmmm," said Coach Blaine with a lamentable lack of originality.

The rain poured down endlessly on the State field, on mud-soaked players and officials, on subs huddled

under waterproofs, and on chilled, drenched spectators.
The game had started in a fine mist, which gradually
grew heavier, and by the second quarter everything
was swamped.

The ball, caked with mud, rested on the State thirty.
The scoreboard was still blank. University supporters,
expecting fireworks from their green-jerseyed candidate for All-American, were doomed to disappoint-
ment, since anything in the fireworks line was apt to
sizzle to the ground as a costly fumble. Soaked, weary
and despairingly unable to score, the two elevens
plowed stubbornly through seas of mud with no ap-
preciable edge on either side.

Skid, needed at half, was holding up fairly well.
Two minutes before the quarter ended, Davis got the
ball and eluded the State secondary by brilliant footwork on the unsure ground.

The University stands were drawn to their feet,
screaming for a touchdown as the University meteor
made it five, ten, fifteen yards . . . Skid caught him by
a superhuman effort on the State ten, and they slid
together into the nearest mud puddle.

Davis got disgustedly to his feet and offered a helping hand. Skid half rose, then sank back with a sharp
exclamation. Doc Hollis picked up his black bag and
scurried onto the field.

Coach Blaine rose and looked along the bench, then
jerked his head toward Nick. "Get in," he said briefly.

A line plunge netted the Big Green a yard; an off-
tackle play, two. With only eight yards to a touchdown, they tried two frantic and ill-timed forward
passes. As Slim knocked down the last, the gun barked

to end the half, and the teams trailed wearily off the field.

In the locker room, Coach Blaine said little, moving quietly from player to player with suggestions and encouragement. The main thing was rest, quiet, and clean uniforms.

"You start at half, Nick," he ordered, just before he left the room.

Nick looked surprised, Ted gave a private cheer, and Steve Harris who had expected to get the nod muttered something under his breath and sank back dispiritedly.

"I told you you'd get a chance some day," said Ted rather untruthfully.

"Yeah, but, Ted—" Nick was worried. "I'm not good enough. I—"

"You will be if you try," said Ted hopefully.

"Bunk," Nick snapped, nerves making him edgy. "You and your eternal preaching about trying! You make me tired."

Bill Baker raised an aching head from his arms and looked at them miserably. They *would* pick a time like this to revive that old fight.

"Pity there isn't some way," said Steve Harris coolly to Nick, "that you can get the University line to fold up for you like Ted did in practice. It would make everything so easy."

"Huh?" said Nick.

Ted got to his feet. "Shut up," he said definitely.

But Steve was just beginning. "Don't tell me little Rollo doesn't know it was you who made him look so good. Don't tell me he thought he'd bowled you over all by his own sweet self?"

Nick shot to his feet and glared at Steve. "That true?" he demanded.

"Ask Ted," Steve suggested, rather uncomfortably.

"Is it, Ted?"

"No, of course it isn't, Nick," said Ted promptly. "I just—" Nick's eyes told him that his story wasn't going to be believed. "Well, I—you—"

Nick glanced around the room. There was concern on nearly every face, but no surprise at Steve's outrageous suggestion. "Everyone seems to have known about this except me," said Nick, too gently.

"Don't be sore, Nick," said Bill, swinging his legs off the rubbing table and sitting up. "Ted just—"

"Yes?"

Bill bit his lip and kept silence.

"What *was* the idea exactly, Ted?" said Nick, still in that quiet voice.

"Well, I—well—" Ted floundered miserably. "Well, darn it, Nick, you'd never try. I knew you could go places, if you cared enough, but you'd just fool around and—quit." He glanced up sharply, but Nick made no comment. "So—well, I thought perhaps if you thought you were really good—well, maybe—"

"As a spell-binder, Ted, you're rotten," said Nick candidly. "You start at the middle and end up at both ends at once. You imbecile," he added dispassionately, "you might have gotten yourself benched."

"Still mad?" said Bill.

Nick glanced sidewise at the captain. "I feel like seven different kinds of a fool, Bill," he said frankly, "and I'd like to kick each one of them separately and hard, but—no—I'm not mad. All right, Ted, I'll play up to your little bromide and TRY. That I should come to this." He heaved a mock-serious sigh. "I suppose I've got to pull a Frank Merriwell now, or never look you guys in the face again."

"*And* stay away from mirrors," Ted agreed cheerfully.

The radio announcer took off his hat and let the water drip out of the brim.

"This is *no* day for football, ladies and gentlemen," he mourned. "Here we are in the fourth quarter of this game between State College and University. No score yet, and it's still pouring. State's been showing more drive this half—Coach Blaine must have plastered on the pep. Number 22—Nicholas Rand—is showing considerable class, and has broken loose twice over his own right guard for long runs. That's number 18—Ted Benedict—who's handing in a fine ball game this afternoon. Ted seems to be engaged in making Nick Rand look good by making the University guard and tackle in there look bad. He's developed a trick of taking out two men at once, and University doesn't like it.

"Well, time out's over. State's ball on their own thirty, with four minutes to go. Here's the play. The shift is to the right. The ball goes to Tubby Green at full. He hits the line hard for—no gain. Maybe a foot. Call it second and ten. There's the signal again—the shift is to the right, and the ball goes to Rand. He's coming around right end, driving in hard and fast up to the thirty-five, the forty, the forty-five . . . He's running hard, plowing through the mud.

"Oh, oh. Beautiful tackle there. Chuck Davis made that tackle, friends, University's white hope for All-American. Wait a minute. . . . Oh, tough luck. Rand fumbled and Davis recovered. University's ball on their own forty-five, first and ten. Rand of State fumbled and Davis recovered for University. This may mean the ball game with only a few minutes to go."

On the field, Bill called for time out. Nick jerked off his helmet and flung it on the ground. "There goes the ball game," he said flatly. "Go on, Ted, make your little speech about trying. It ought to come in good right here."

"Quitting before the five o'clock whistle, aren't you?" said Ted.

"Oh, cut out that quitting talk!" Nick snapped. "This dying for dear old State is a lot of bunk—dying or trying, I don't care which."

"Short, short story," said Ted. "Chuck Davis, All-American. Nicholas Rand, alias All-American. That's just the difference."

"I couldn't help that fumble," Nick began defensively.

"Oh, go to blazes!" Ted jerked out. "Who said you could? We've got two minutes left and anything can happen. But you just don't care, and it's all right with me. I'm sick to death of trying to get you to play ball. I'm through."

The referee's whistle sheared through Nick's jumbled thoughts.

"Number 11 for University at full. No gain. Second and still ten to go." The announcer picked up the thread of the play. "The ball is on University's forty-five. Here's the play—it's a spinner, but it looks like they've caught the man back of the line. No, I'm wrong." The announcer's voice rose sharply. "It was a fake. Chuck Davis has the ball—he's running wide around his own left end. He's cutting in. His interference is forming beautifully. He's at the forty, the thirty, the twenty-five— It looks like a touchdown! State's safety man is waiting on the six-yard line. Davis is scooting down field like a thunderbolt. Mehaffey's set for him — He's got him! Mehaffey stopped the University comet on the eight-yard line. Boy oh boy!"

He paused to catch his breath.

"University's ball on the eight, first down and goal to go. Only one minute left. There's the play—straight line plunge. No gain—State's digging in. Second and goal to go. Oh, oh, they lost a yard on that one. Bad pass from center and the ball was free for a moment. What'll it be—a forward pass over the goal line? It's third down with nine yards to go for that score.

"Here it comes. Incomplete over the goal line. Fourth and still nine. The timekeeper's got his gun out. This is going to be a mighty close thing. Here's the play—shift to the right. Davis is fading back—it's another high pass. And it's incomplete. . . . No, it isn't! A State man has intercepted! He's coming out fast from behind the goal line. . . . He's up to the ten, the fifteen, the twenty . . . He's boxed in on the thirty—looks like he's caught. No, he's loose again. I can't see his number, but he's sure in there trying. He's up at midfield with the whole University team on his heels. State interference had no time to form. He's leading the pack . . . he's loose . . . I think

. . . He's on the University thirty, the twenty— He's OVER! It's a touchdown! a touchdown for State!— and there's the gun! Ladies and gentlemen, it's a touchdown and the conference title for State College. Gosh." He backed up and sat down in a state of near collapse on the sound technician's hat.

Nick lay across the goal line where he had fallen and hugged the ball to him. It was shapeless with caked mud, but at the moment he loved it dearly. Maybe if he tried very hard, he could stand up. Try! There it was again. Oh, well. Anyhow, he thought wearily, struggling to his feet, he wouldn't be apt to regard football as just a game again. It *was* a game, a swell game, but he'd fought for that last fifty yards like a wild man.

Two years later on the University field, a scrub halfback studied his part in a complicated fake pass play. University faced State the following Saturday, and they wanted vengeance. The scrub grinned contentedly. His was the stellar part in the day's scrimmage. He was alias Nicholas Rand.

THE MAGNIFICENT
MERGER

"Good? He's too good! I've known him three years and he's told me many times!" Ted Dale stood in the tent doorway and wailed in a minor key. "Everything anyone else does, he does better. But I haven't seen him lately and maybe he's changed— I don't think . . . We will *not* pass inspection, William, if you sweep the dust under the bed."

"What do you care?" sad Bill Rhodes amiably. "It's my bed. Besides it's as good there as outdoors and it doesn't make the doorstep dusty." He drove home his point by making a flourish with the broom and knocking Ted's flashlight off its stand.

Ted gave a howl and leaped inside the tent. "If you've broken that—" he shrieked indignantly.

"Oh, forget it," Bill urged. "Accidents will happen."

"They do," Ted agreed bitterly, "especially when you're around. You'd better step gently when the Merger comes."

"The what?" said Bill.

217

"The Merger. He was too good for one fellow, so he merged." There was no dawn of intelligence on Bill's placid countenance, and Ted frowned. "Merge—incorporate—consolidate—like companies do," he enlarged.

"Oh," said Bill, "I see."

"Good for you," Ted murmured gently. "You know, I feel my feeble witticisms would go over better if they didn't have to be explained."

"They'd go over better if you didn't make them," Bill suggested unkindly. "When does this Merger arrive?"

"Any minute. I was watching for him. That's why I was standing outside, breathing deeply."

"Oh, was that why?" Bill snorted. "And me thinking you were avoiding the sweeping. I misjudged you, Ted. I'm sorry." He affected great emotion and turned away with heaving shoulders.

"My pal!" Ted remarked abstractedly. "I see a cloud of dust approaching—must be the Merger. What a speed-demon *he* is."

Bill laid down his broom and peered at a languid youth, laden with suitcases. "Is that the Merger?" he said in awe.

"It is, and it's going to merge in with us and take up a third of the space. When I think," Teddy became heated, "that, out of sixty-two fellows, we got that, I could—"

"Shut up," said Bill abruptly and dashed out of the tent to welcome the new arrival. "You *are* Prescott Stewart, aren't you?" he asked admiringly.

The Merger nodded. "*The* Prescott Stewart," he admitted.

"That's what I meant," said Bill humbly, gazing at the distinguished visitor. Naturally one knew all about Prescott Stewart, crack athlete of Morrill High, the home of champions. Bill made faint gurgling noises. "I hope you'll like it here," he said anxiously.

The Merger stepped inside the tent and dropped his suitcases. "Don't think I shall," he commented, "but I suppose it'll have to do. Are you Rhodes?"

"Yes. Bill Rhodes. You know Ted Dale, don't you?"

Ted looked at the newcomer indifferently. " 'Lo, Prescott. How are you?" he acknowledged. "Which bed do you want?"

Bill interrupted feebly. "But, Ted, this is *Prescott* Stewart. You didn't tell me."

"Don't be dumb," said Ted. "I know it is." He turned to the Merger. "Swimming, too, isn't it? I've heard something about your racing—"

"I swim," said the Merger modestly, expanding his chest a trifle.

"Yes," Ted agreed patiently.

"I play tennis, too," the Merger added, his tone indicating that he was understating the case.

"Yes." Ted's voice was even more patient.

"And I—"

"What do you want to be called?" Ted interrupted hastily. "Prescott's too darned lengthy."

"Everyone calls me Speed now," said the Merger complacently. "It's more suitable and it's quite a trademark."

"Speed?" Ted ejaculated unbelievingly.

"Why, yes." The Merger explained it painstakingly.

"I'm a ten-second man in the century, State record in the hurdles—"

He showed signs of going on, but Ted interrupted again. "Would you mind if I called you Merge?"

"What? How do you spell it?"

Ted started to answer, but Bill forestalled him. "M-E-R-J," he sputtered. "It's a—er—Norwegian word meaning—er—athletic." Ted snorted, and turned his back to open a drawer.

"Oh." The Merger accepted the explanation condescendingly. "Why, no, that's all right. I guess I'm an athlete in any language." He frowned. "On second thought, though, I'd rather be called Speed. Everyone knows Speed Stewart."

Ted turned, sober as a judge. "Okay. Speed it is. Hello there, Spud."

Spud Davis entered the tent hesitatingly, and Bill introduced the Merger.

"What do you want?" said Ted impatiently.

"I came to borrow your alarm clock," Spud murmured, his round face expressing pleasure at meeting the great Prescott Stewart.

"Why an alarm clock?" Ted inquired.

"To put under Dutch's pillow, so I won't have to wear myself out waking him. If that doesn't work, I'll try ice water."

"But I need my clock."

"Ever tried to wake Dutch up?" Spud asked. Ted nodded.

"Well, then," triumphantly, "you ought to know how I need that clock. Be a pal," he urged.

"All right," said Ted resignedly. "Here it is." He handed over the battered timepiece with a sigh.

Spud seized it eagerly. "Thanks—I'll be seeing you. So long, Stewart—awfully glad to have met you."

"Goodbye, Procrastination," said Ted darkly.

"What'd you call me?" Spud stood uncertainly in the doorway, swinging the clock in his fingers.

"Procrastination."

"But why?" Spud protested.

"Procrastination is the thief of time," Ted explained triumphantly. "Nix! Don't throw that clock at me, you goofus. Scram!"

Spud gave a wail of despair and fled, but a moment later he was back in the doorway. "Did I leave my knife here?" he asked, stepping inside.

"This it?" Ted picked a knife up from a box.

"Thanks." Spud pocketed it gratefully and turned to go. The Merger was immediately galvanized into action. "Wait," he protested.

"Huh?"

"Sit down and count ten," the Merger ordered. "Don't you know it's bad luck to come back for anything, unless you sit down and count ten?"

"Nerts," Ted remarked.

"But it's perfectly true," the Merger insisted indignantly. Spud looked at him in surprise, decided he was joking and walked out of the tent. The Merger made a gesture of despair. "He's in for trouble," he prophesied gloomily. "But I warned him. I—" He broke off. Through the doorway, they saw Spud stumble on a root and fall squarely into a mud puddle. The Merger nodded, almost with satisfaction.

Spud picked himself up wrathfully, and Ted immediately burst forth:

That person is Davis the Great-o,
He had a most terrible fate-o;
For, being named Spud,
He fell in the mud,
And thus he became a Potato.

Spud wiped mud off his face and glared at the poet. "Wait till I get scraped off, and I'll give you something to laugh about." Then he chortled. "I'm afraid your clock's a bit muddy, Ted," and fled with Ted in hot pursuit.

Bill turned to the Merger. "Do you really believe that stuff?" he asked incredulously.

"It isn't stuff," the Merger began hotly, then laughed. "Well, I used to think so myself," he admitted, "before the Brackett High baseball game. I didn't think we had a chance in the world to win, but I found a four-leaf clover and a horseshoe, and during the game I picked up a pin."

"Well, what happened?" said Bill.

"We won, of course," said the Merger, surprised at the question. "I pitched! The other team never had a chance."

Bill digested this information in silence, then changed the subject. "You're in time for Field Day," he said, "and I should think you might get the All-Around Cup."

"Athletics?" said the Merger. "Might? That's right up my alley? Where do I sign?"

On their way to the Camp Office, they ran into Ted returning, hot and disheveled, from his argument. "Spud was right about Dutch's sleeping," he admitted. "We rolled all over the tent and the big dodo never wiggled. My dear old clock'll wear out. Gosh, it's hot. I'm going swimming."

"Be right with you," said Bill. "Speed's signing up for the All-Around."

"Oh, Speed is?" said Ted oddly. "Good enough. Righto, I'll meet you in the sweet bye-and-bye."

"You'll meet us in the lake," Bill corrected, and left hurriedly.

On the beach fifteen minutes later, Ted opened one eye and looked up lazily at Bill and Speed. "I thought you were going swimming," Speed objected, prodding Ted with his foot.

"Ouch," said Ted, rolling away and sitting up, "I *was,* but the water was too cold."

Bill thrust in an experimental foot and withdrew it with a yelp. "Boy, I'll say it's cold!" he howled. "Feels like the Arctic in midwinter." He noticed Speed on the diving board. "You going to dive in? You great, big, wonderful he-man, you! Well, go on, why don't you?"

Speed obliged with a beautiful racing dive, and Bill drew a deep breath and plunged. Ted nibbled thoughtfully at a blade of grass, then walked to the water's edge. "Come on in," Bill shouted cheerfully, splashing water about like a porpoise. "The water feels fine."

"I don't doubt it does," Ted conceded, "but *I* don't. I feel blamed cold. Oh well, here goes." He went under and came up spluttering. "Race you to the raft!"

They started level, but Speed streaked ahead, and pulled himself onto the raft long before their hands touched the wood. "Gosh," said Bill admiringly, "your nickname sure fits."

Speed shrugged his shoulders. "I hold quite a few cups for sprints, of course—"

"You do just about everything, don't you?"

"Just about," said Speed smugly. "I'm afraid I won't get much competition here. Or have you some *good* swimmers?"

Bill flushed. He was considered one of the best athletes in the camp, and to be classed as poor was dampening to his spirits. Ted answered for him. "Quite a few, I believe. You'll get competition all right." He smiled sweetly and slid off the raft. Speed dived and, when Ted's feet touched the beach, Speed was beside him. Bill turned up breathlessly a moment later.

"Bit winded?" Speed inquired patronizingly, then dashed forward with a cry to pick something out of the grass. "A four-leaf clover," he exulted. "Best luck in the world. Watch my smoke now."

"Do you really believe that?" Ted asked.

"Of course I do," Speed snapped. "Didn't Spud flop in the mud after—"

"Bunk!" said Ted. "He's always falling over his feet."

"No, it was because he came back—"

"Rats," Ted snorted, then suddenly changed the subject. "Did you sign up?" Speed nodded sulkily. Ted tried another tack. "Race you to the tent," he suggested, and this time his peaceful overtures were more successful. Speed beat them both by a matter of yards.

"It comes to this," said Tom Thurman impressively. "Your Speed pal has spoiled the whole show. He's a great athlete—I admit it—but Field Day's going to be a frost, if he annexes everything. And the way he talks about himself—you'd think he was Achilles."

All the boys in the group nodded solemn agreement. They were sitting on the beach, a week after Speed's arrival, watching stars. "You said it," said Spud. "Why not give him the Cup and just have a runner-up competition?" He nudged Ted irritably. "Come on, grandpa, think of something. All you do is lie there and stare at the sky."

"That's Orion," said Ted conversationally.

"Hang the stars," said Dutch. "And it's Mars anyhow. What about Speed?"

"It's Orion," said Ted firmly. "Admit that, and I'll put my brain to work on this trifling question of yours."

"Oh, all right, all right—Jupiter, if you like, but crank up the thinking apparatus."

"Not Jupiter," Ted repeated patiently. "Orion. Now, what was it?" He looked about the group innocently. "About the Merger?"

"Merj—great Norwegian athlete," Tom corrected. "Think of some way to save the day."

"Don't talk in rhymes—it makes my head spin. Let's see." Ted stared pensively at the lake. "How about—" he began, but broke off suddenly.

Speed stepped out from the shadows and greeted the group.

Ted looked up innocently. "Isn't that star Orion?"

"How should I know? I never bother with stars." Speed sat on a convenient stump and looked at the sky with disapproval.

"Being a star athlete yourself, I suppose?" said Tom with gentle sarcasm.

"Perhaps." Speed accepted the compliment composedly. "Say, isn't that a new moon?" Several nodded. "And I'm not looking through glass or trees. Here, quick, give me a dime." Bill produced the required bit of silver, which Speed seized eagerly, turning it in his hand and then pocketing it.

"Hey," said Bill.

"Oh, I'll pay you back," Speed assured him. "But not with this dime. Don't you know that, if you turn your money over when you see a new moon, it's lucky and you get rich?"

"Unlucky for Bill, I should say," Dutch murmured.

There was a rustle in the bushes behind them, and a dignified black cat stalked majestically into their midst. "Meow," said the cat.

"Meow," said Bill fraternally. "Where'd you come from?"

"It's just visiting," Ted offered lazily. "What's the trouble, Speed? You look as if you'd seen a ghost."

"But it's black," Speed exclaimed.

"Sure, it is." The cat walked toward Speed affectionately, and Speed backed away to prevent its crossing his path, finally turning in desperation and making for the tents.

"Well!" Tom voiced the sentiments of the entire company. "Well, well . . . Where were we?"

"You were saying that Speed's too good at athletics," said Ted. "And so he is, which wouldn't matter if he didn't keep saying so. I had a lecture yesterday on how he won the city championship in tiddley-winks. But never mind." He paused impressively. "Leave it to Uncle Theodore. Uncle has an idea." He gazed at the sky complacently. "Orion is certainly a beautiful star," he murmured.

"Mars," said Dutch, "and it's a planet."

"Steady on your marks, boys," Mr. Peabody, the camp director, warned and raised his starter's gun. Speed wriggled impatiently, and Tom and Dutch dug deeper into starting holes.

"Great athlete, that Stewart," said a spectator audibly, and Speed nodded agreement, well pleased.

"Go!" The runners shot forward into the open, Speed ahead. He ran so effortlessly that Tom, ordinarily an excellent quarter-miler, lost ground in admiration. Dutch strained to the limit but could not compete with those flying heels. Speed smiled confidently and glanced ahead at the track, wondering how easily he could take it. A black object minced over the rough cinders. Speed slowed up and glared at the visiting cat with wrath. "Shoo," he said unconvincingly, slowing up more as it became clear that the animal intended to cross.

"Shoo," he repeated. The cat stopped in its journey and purred inquiringly. Speed made for the outside edge in the hope of foiling the cat's apparent intention of crossing his path. The cat followed lovingly and the onlookers roared. Dutch took the lead and Speed, with a desperate lunge, nosed out the cat by an inch and cut the corner in front of its waving whiskers.

The crowd applauded as Dutch and Tom breasted the tape together, the cat episode having given them the lead. Speed came in, puffing angrily, to demand that the race be run over again.

Mr. Peabody eyed him with surprise. "My dear boy," he protested, "you could have jumped that cat."

"But it would have gone in front of me then. I ought to have won," he mourned, then shrugged his shoulders and turned away. "Oh, well," he murmured, "no one else entered for everything. I'll win the dives and swimming easy enough."

"Oh sure," said Ted, coming up behind him.

Jack Logan stood on the dock and watched Speed complete one faultless practice dive after another. "What's the good of my trying?" he asked Ted bitterly. "Look at that guy!"

Ted patted him on the back and sauntered to the diving board with a broad grin on his face. Speed came up dripping, and Ted greeted him enthusiastically. "Great diving," he said heartily. "Say, look what I found for you." He held out a bit of green, which Speed accepted curiously. "A four-leaf clover," said Ted proudly.

Speed stared in horror. "Great guns!" he exclaimed. "Don't you know it's the worst luck in the world to give anyone a four-leaf clover? They're no good unless you find them yourself. Give five-leaf's for luck, but not four's. You've ruined everything, you idiot."

Ted stared bewilderedly. "I'm sorry," he began. "I

had no idea." Then he burst out laughing. "Heck, Speed, you don't really believe that stuff?"

"Of course I do," Speed fumed, "and it isn't stuff. The last time anyone gave me a four-leaf clover, I knocked over three hurdles in a race and got myself disqualified."

"Well, give it back," said Ted with a resigned sigh.

"What good would that do? It's too late now. Of all the chumps," Speed muttered, putting the clover on the dock. "Well, never mind. I'm too good to lose."

Mr. Peabody lined the diving contestants up on the platform. "Running swan," he ordered efficiently, and Dutch launched into the air in a good dive. He was followed by Jack, then Bill, and others. Finally Speed stepped coolly to the board.

"Show 'em how, big boy!" shouted an admirer, and Speed smiled and raised a hand in acknowledgment. Then he gave an odd leap, a convulsive wriggle and floundered awkwardly into the water. He came up spluttering, and the judges chorused "Very poor" and issued instructions for the next dive.

Speed pulled himself onto the dock and sat down by Bill and Ted to glare at divers, judges and audience impartially.

"Haven't you ever done a running swan before?" Bill ventured innocently.

"Of course I have," Speed exploded, "hundreds of times. A bee bit me."

"Bees don't bite," said Ted sweetly. "They sting."

"It was all that darned clover," Speed growled, staring at it in impotent rage.

"But the bee wasn't on the clover," Ted protested reasonably. "I *know* he wasn't, or he'd have stung me. Bees always do."

"You know perfectly well what I mean." Speed lapsed into a sulky silence and, when his turn came again, did a half-hearted double somersault with a haunted look on his face even in mid-air.

The judges finally gave first place to Jack, whereupon Speed pulled the clover into bits and threw it in the lake.

"Tut, tut," said Ted reproachfully. "I thought you won things because you were an athlete."

"Shut up," said Speed savagely. "I *do* win things because I'm good. I can beat anyone here with both hands tied behind my back, but I can't beat luck like this."

"Okay," said Ted. "Are you in the swimming race, or are you all worn out by your encounters with Lady Luck?"

"Go sit on a tack," Speed invited and stalked off in search of less captious company.

An odd thing happened during the swimming race. A large camp banner on the diving platform worked loose and was dangling perilously over the water, when Ted volunteered to fix it. He put a ladder from the float to the platform and, with Tom and Spud hanging valiantly at the bottom, climbed upwards. The ladder itself, bridging as it did the gap between float and platform, also reached over the established course of the race.

It was too much for Speed. He slowed the beat of

his powerful crawl stroke, hesitated, then went around. As one of the judges remarked later, it was just as well that Speed came in last, because he really had not followed the prescribed course.

It was Bill who tried to soothe the seething Merger and led him off to change into tennis clothes and complete the competition. Inside the tent, Speed sank wearily into a chair and groaned.

"It's tough all right," Bill sympathized.

"What do you care?" Speed snapped at him. "You won the swimming race, didn't you? And I could beat you, swimming backwards and tied to an anchor! But I'm going to lick Ted in the tennis matches if it's the last thing I do. I'll run him ragged—him and his clovers!"

"I'm sorry about that," said Ted from the doorway. "I didn't know about clovers. Say, aren't you sitting on my book?"

"I don't know and I don't care," said Speed wrathfully.

"No, but I care. Get up, there's a good guy. Get off it."

Speed leaped up, snatched the book and flung it wildly through the doorway. Ted frowned and went outside, returning a moment later with the book and several fragments of glass, which he handed to Bill. "It's that pocket mirror of yours," he said apologetically. "I'm sorry. I shouldn't have used it as a bookmark."

Speed leaped again to his feet. "Mirror?" he demanded. "Mirror? Oh, for the love of mud—seven years' bad luck! You can have the cup and everything else!" He stamped out of the tent and would have slammed the door, except that there was no door to slam.

"I'm sorry," said Mr. Peabody benignly, "but we can't give the cup this year. No one got more than one first place." He stepped back and bumped into Speed. "Ah, Prescott," he said genially, "I expected *you* to walk off with all the honors."

"I was unlucky," Speed said. "A black cat and a broken mirror and everything else. Could I beat that combination?"

"My dear boy," Mr. Peabody began in a shocked voice, "no one nowadays—" He paused to peer at Speed, then laughed. "Well, well, for one moment I thought you were in earnest. Very good, very good indeed." He went off, laughing heartily, and Speed stared after him and gritted his teeth.

Ted stopped by consolingly. "Well, if you didn't get it, neither did anyone else."

"I was—" Speed stopped.

"Unlucky." Ted finished it for him. "And here I thought you were really good at all these things—"

"I *am* good," said Speed. "Everyone knows I'm good."

"So I've heard," said Ted. "You'd give Napoleon an inferiority complex. Only, Napoleon didn't blame things on luck. Honestly, why don't you get wise to yourself? You didn't lose because of bad luck, you nut. If you'd jumped over that cat and gone under the ladder, you'd have won. You lost because you *didn't* go under the ladder—because the cat *didn't* cross your path. And you weren't the one who broke the mirror. *I* knocked it off the table, so if there's seven years' bad luck coming, it's mine. And you'll never know what a whale of a time it took to find a five-leafed clover, so I could tear one leaf off."

Speed stared in stricken astonishment. "Then it wasn't just luck?"

"Luck your grandmother!" Ted snorted. "The only luck you've had is that no one's knocked your block off, when you've been yapping about what a great athlete you are."

"But I *am*," said Speed.

"Not if you win on luck," Ted told him with finality. "You're just a big bust."

Speed stared uncertainly. "I *am* a good athlete, I'm one of the best in the state," he began belligerently, then trailed off. "Maybe I was kind of dumb to be so—so superstitious, if those things were fakes."

"O-kay." Ted snapped his fingers. "I admit you're good, and you admit you're dumb. The age of miracles is not yet over." He walked off, leaving Speed to stare after him open-mouthed.

There was only one more comment on the matter.

"I see another big merger has gone bust," Ted said casually at dinner that evening. Speed reached for the bread tray and knocked over a salt-cellar.

"Throw some over your left shoulder," Ted advised. "It's bad luck to spill salt."

Speed instinctively reached out a hand, then drew it back, and began to butter his bread. "What were you saying about a merger?" he asked.

Ted whistled softly between his teeth. "I was just saying that another big merger has submerged," he answered. "But," he added, "it's beginning to emerge, and it may pay dividends yet."

THE WINNER

I REMEMBER the first time I ever saw Steve Kennedy play tennis.

I was sitting in front of the East Side tennis house, waiting for my turn to get out on the clay and beat the stuffing out of Bud Mueller. Bud was explaining very kindly that I was living in a dream world.

"I shall beat you six-zero and six-one," he said generously. "The one game you win is to keep up your morale."

"Kind of you," I said, peaceful in the knowledge that my backhand had recently taken a turn for the superlative. "Who's the new guy on court five?"

"Dunno." Bud screwed up his eyes against the sun. "Nice drive."

I nodded. The drive was wicked.

The new guy in question was a rangy customer with dark hair, a long-arm reach and a pair of feet that moved like a ballet dancer's. Wherever the ball went, he was under it, and when he socked it back, it kicked up hard little spurts of dust. He was playing against a little

dynamo named Joe Hughes, a tough, red-headed youngster with a lot of endurance and occasional attacks of
brilliance. Joe had a hard accurate drive but was weak
at the net, and the new guy was making the most of it.

Even then—and that was before I knew Steve Kennedy's name or anything about him—I noticed the way
he blasted for every point like he was dynamite in a
mountain. This was supposed to be a friendly, pick-up
game, but you'd have thought Steve was pitching for
Forest Hills or Wimbledon. For my money, it was too
hot to work that hard.

I yelled at one of the fellows who had just come out
of the tennis house. "Who's the new guy, Tommy?"

Tommy came bounding over like a junior Winchell.
"That's Steve Kennedy," he said. "He's from California."

I said, "Oh."

"He's got a lot of tennis cups," Tommy went on,
"and he won the park championship in his district, and
then his family moved here or he could have played
for the city title. Speed Wilton was his coach."

I'd heard of Speed Wilton, of course. Who hasn't?
That accounted for some of the prettiest drives and
overhead smashes I'd ever seen. I said, "Well. Where'd
you get all the dope, Thomas?"

"From Steve. He's a nice guy. I'll bet he walks off
with the city title here, one of these days."

Bud said, "He tell you that too?"

"Well, he asked what the competition was like."

I said, "Oh" again. I was in a sort of conversational
rut, but that was because my attention was on this Kennedy character, who interested me a whole lot. Just at

that moment, he took the game off Joe with a beautifully paced dink shot and walked to the baseline.

Bud whacked me on the back and told me to get a
move on. I said, "Wait a minute. I want to watch this
guy serve." Bud growled, but I didn't care. I was watching Steve Kennedy. He used a flat service, hitting the
ball with the racket face open. His timing was beautiful, and Joe's stabbing effort to handle the shot was a
feeble pop-up. Steve blitzed the return and took the
point.

I said, "Well!" Then Bud started encouraging me
with his racket from the rear, and I said, "Okay, okay,"
and moved on. "Just the same," I told him, "that guy's
good. He's going to be heard from."

"*I'm* going to be heard from," Bud howled, "unless you get going. I didn't come here to watch California cavort." So I shut him up in two sets, 6-3 and
6-2, which he said was unethical, illegal and revolting.

After that, I saw Steve around a good deal, and it was
always the same story. He took practice games like
anyone else would take tournament play, even when the
heat was so bad that I felt myself as if I was swimming
around in slow-motion soup. And he was very, very
good.

I thought, a couple of times, that I'd go over and suggest a rally together, but for some reason I didn't. And
then, one afternoon, I was lying on a bench at the courts
when a voice said, "You're Bill Wheelock, aren't you?"

I admitted it and said, "You're Steve Kennedy."
He admitted that, and there we were, officially introduced.

"You waiting for someone?"

I nodded. "Bud Mueller. He probably tangled with a malted milk or got lost in a coke. Bud trains the hard way."

Steve grinned. "I heard you're pretty good."

Not from me he hadn't heard that. I know what my game needs, and it's plenty. I said modestly that they were after me for the Davis Cup team, but otherwise I was strictly a cipher. Steve's grin spread around a bit, pleasantly. "Care to try a rally with me, just until our partners show up?"

I said sure. And, right there, I got really interested in Steve Kennedy's career, because in about two minutes I knew I'd been right when I told Bud the guy was going places. He had everything a tennis player needs —a drive as clean and straight as a willow stick, a really fine backhand, a chop stroke that was a curse to handle, and a high-voltage smash.

But we were only supposed to be rallying—set-'em-up-and-push-'em-over—and Steve never once fluffed a point. In fact, twice, he cut the clay out from under my feet with blackjack shots. After about fifteen minutes of that, under a hot sun, you could have poured me down the nearest drain.

I figured that, if I wanted to be in circulation when Bud showed up, I'd better retire. I caught Steve's last drive in my hand—and I might add that it stung—walked over to the net, picked up my towel and started mopping-up operations. Steve looked surprised but strolled over to join me. "See your partner coming for your match?"

I shook my head. "Nope. Thought I'd better quit before I had a lily in my hand.—You really play marbles for keeps, don't you?"

"How do you mean?"

"Well, I—gee, after all, it's only a rally. I mean, who cares who gets the point?"

Steve said seriously, "*I* care."

That sort of stopped me. Up to then, I guess I'd been figuring it was a reflex action. I started, "But, for the love of Mike—" and he interrupted me. "I make it a habit to win," he said.

I looked at him. He was standing there, spinning his racket, and he didn't look like a guy who was too big for his boots. He looked nice and easy. "Don't you?" he asked politely.

"Don't I what?"

"Play to win?"

I thought about it for a second, and then I shook my head.

"What *do* you play for, then?"

He asked the darnedest questions. "Well—fun, exercise. Because I like the game."

"Don't you go in for tournament play at all?"

I said that I did and added that I'd been in the city quarter-finals the year before, although I'd only entered because the rest of our bunch had and tournament play is good for a tennis game. You learn a lot. I told Steve that, and his eyebrows went up, but he said easily, "Well, that's the difference between you and me, then. When I enter a tournament, I intend to win it."

He jerked his head toward the court. "Look, if you don't like wrestling for points, how about feeding each other shots on our weak strokes?" He grinned at me. "I'm a good boy when I'm practicing, especially on my weak shots, so please help me out."

I grinned back. I couldn't help it. "You got any weak shots?"

"Umm. Stop-volleys at the net, for one thing. Want to be a good Samaritan?"

I said yes, but it wasn't just noble impulses that made me start tossing the kind of balls he wanted. I knew class when I saw it, and some day Steve Kennedy was going to be a big name in tennis. Having a player from our own clubhouse turn up some day in the national junior finals would be all right with me. I'd known for a long time how far I'd go myself. It wasn't that far.

So that was how it started. That was how I got the habit of spending a lot of my time building up a guy I knew some day would be at the top. It riled Bud a little, because we missed some of our afternoon sessions, but I knew what I was doing. As a matter of fact, it didn't hurt my own tennis. My backhand got strengthened, and when he used American twist serves I learned to take them as they came. And I even developed a reasonable amount of brightness in reaching his deceptive drop shot and raking his chop strokes off the ground.

We worked hard that month, and I got to like Steve a lot. One thing about him bothered me some, but one thing wasn't much. I've got enough dopey features of my own, and I figure if I can get along with me I can get along with anybody. If winning games meant so much to Steve Kennedy—well, that was just Steve's way of looking at things.

He signed up for the clubhouse tournament the same day I did. We both went into the semi-finals, and then I had a bad afternoon and lost a 3-2 match to Donny Carlson. That's an alibi and I don't like alibis, but I was really off my shots that day. It happens to every tennis player; there'll be one afternoon when your racket doesn't fit your hand, the net jumps up in the air to catch your shots, and the court trips you when you're running for a high one. That was me against Donny, and I figured okay, better luck next time.

So Steve played an Irish kid named McCarthy for the title, and they put on an exhibition that had the gallery clawing at its hair. McCarthy hits 'em where they ain't, like baseball's Willy Keeler, and Steve had to lay himself out all the time. McCarthy actually had him 2-all with set point against him, 'vantage in.

When Steve walked back to receive what could have been the last serve in the match, he made me think of a leopard waiting to jump out of a tree. You could almost feel him harden and settle inside himself. McCarthy tried to ace him on the first serve, and the shot was a ribbon-tagged honey. It lay down so flat in the dust that it should have taken a knife to get under it, but Steve's racket head wedged in and lofted it back. McCarthy stretched for a volley, ceiling zero, but the damage to the Irish was done and the return was jam for Steve. He didn't just kill the ball, he murdered it, and the umpire said "Deuce" with an admiring gasp.

McCarthy had thrown everything he had into the last effort, and, in spite of himself, he leveled off. Steve didn't. He took the points he needed, and they crowned a new club champion. A good one.

But, looking back, what I remembered about that match was afterwards. It was, literally, hours before Steve could get unwound. He couldn't sit down and relax; he couldn't even eat dinner. His bedsprings that night must really have taken a beating.

And why?

Because he'd almost lost.

I tried to kid him out of it and remind him that tennis was only a game and not a full-scale war, but he snapped at me and I quit. Only, having gotten myself mixed up in the guy's career, I couldn't keep my mouth shut indefinitely, and the next day I led with my chin.

Steve and I had a long workout that afternoon, and I realized again that he had all the stuff it takes to make him top-flight. Except one thing. He didn't know how to lose and he cared too blamed much about victory. And that was going to add up to trouble, because champions learn to take the lickings as they come. That's why they're champions.

I eased into it gradually. I asked Steve if he was going to enter for the city title, knowing perfectly well he would because the entry of a club champion is almost automatic. I was entering myself, and I was only a runner-up.

Steve said, sure. I said cautiously, "Well, don't knock yourself out like you did yesterday. There's other years."

He gave me a funny look. He said, "You're back on that subject, are you, Bill? What have you got against a guy winning his games?"

I said I didn't have anything against it. All I meant was there was such a thing as caring too much. It made you lose track of a lot of things that were just as important.

"Such as what?" said Steve.

I said flatly, "Such as playing the game for its own sake."

Steve said, "Ah, nuts." I can't say I blamed him. If anyone ever sounded like dear old corn-fed Grandpa in a flat spin, it was certainly yours truly. After all, Steve's game was Steve's business, not mine. I told myself to skip it, and that's what I did until the day he played Joe Weiss, and I found out that there are some things you can't skip.

That was in the city tournament, and both Steve and I were still in the running. It was no credit to me. The draws had been all in my favor, but Steve had really earned his wins. My feeling that he would be a tennis great some day was turning into a conviction.

I didn't have a match on that afternoon so I was watching from the sidelines. Steve's opponent was a youngster named Joe Weiss, just a little blond kid with not much style. Certainly he didn't show anything in that first set, and Steve took it, 6-2. Right there, I guess he decided it would be a walkover, and besides the weather was rotten. It was one of those sultry days when the climate comes and sits on your chest.

Steve eased off a little—unusual for Steve, but anyone would have said it was a safe bet. Easing off, he still took the second set, 6-3. One more, and the match was his in a walk.

Only it turned out that Joe Weiss was a money player, one of those tennis boys who never really put the pressure on until they're up against a wall. He played way over his head, and the third set was his.

Steve's no quitter; he steadied. But, once the tension has been off a player, it's next to impossible to get it back again, and Joe was just hitting his stride. He pulled up to two sets all, when a nice crisp drive off Steve's racket tripped on the net and fell back, instead of rolling over for the point.

I found myself thinking that maybe I'd know now what happened to Steve Kennedy when he lost.

Steve took the first game of that last set, and Joe took the next two. You could tell yourself that Steve was much the better player, but that didn't change the score. Lady Luck was riding with Joe Weiss, and the breaks went his way.

So the games were 2-1 when it happened. Joe was serving, and the score was 30-40. If Steve took that game, it would even things at 2-all. If he lost it, he'd be really in trouble, with a 3-1 lead for Joe. Steve wanted that point.

He wanted it too darned much.

Joe served—nothing remarkable. Steve drove it cross-court. It came flying back as if someone had taped wings on the cover. Steve's return was loaded with top-spin, and Joe slammed into it with more enthusiasm than accuracy. The shot looked as if it would go wide, but somehow it stayed in, just clipping the line.

Steve, out of position, turned and raced for it. It was a shot that nobody could get, and he got it. He got it by plunging headlong for the ball and, as he fell, stabbing wildly with his racket. By rights, the return should have gone into the net or the gallery or the umpire's chair, but miracles do happen occasionally. The shot fell fair in Joe's court.

It couldn't, of course, have been an easier set-up for Joe to handle. Steve was wide open for a kill, and the ball was high and soft and just asking for it. But Joe slung his racket lightly down and under and floated back a gentleman's lob, giving Steve all the time in the world to recover.

It was a toss-away shot, done courteously to get the ball back in action again without either side benefiting from Steve's fall.

Steve didn't see it that way. He was back on his feet and all set, and he smashed down on that ball with every ounce of drive in him. It torpedoed over the net and flattened out in Joe's court.

I heard the umpire say expressionlessly, "Game to Kennedy. The games are now 2-all." I saw Joe Weiss's face go perfectly blank. I didn't even look at Steve.

I got to my feet. I didn't care who won the match, or whether anybody won it. I'd found out—but good!— how much Steve Kennedy cared about winning.

I had a match myself the next day, which I won. Steve was on the sidelines, and he came over when play ended. The sick, disappointed feeling I'd had when he smashed Joe Weiss's easy lob was still inside me, and I knew the edge in my voice showed it. By that time I'd added it up pretty simply—I'd been wrong about the kind of guy Steve Kennedy was, and the best thing to do was cut my losses. I knew for sure that I wasn't going to spend any more time setting them up for that kind of a winning game.

Steve said, "Hi, Bill," and I said, "Hello" and went on walking. He grabbed my elbow. "What's your hurry?"

I shrugged him off. He'd have had to be blind, deaf and dumb not to know I was sore, but he acted like everything was normal. "Practise with me tomorrow morning?" he said.

There it was, laid out on the line. I said, "No."

"Why not?"

Well, he knew "why not" as well as I did, so I didn't answer.

Steve said, flat and stiff, "You didn't like my taking that point off Joe Weiss yesterday."

He'd asked for it. I snapped, "No, I didn't, since you want to know. It's not *my* idea of tennis."

"It was perfectly legal."

I agreed. "A lot of things are perfectly legal in this world," I said. "That doesn't mean I have to like them."

There was a short silence. Then Steve said, "Does that mean no more practise together?" I nodded, and he looked at me queerly and went on. "You told me once you liked my game and that you didn't mind working overtime to build a champion. You change your mind, Bill?"

I said no. I said I'd still work to build a champion. I said, "You'll never be a champion."

His eyes went flinty. "What do you mean?"

"Just exactly what you think I mean. You haven't got what it takes." I didn't want to talk about it any more. I walked away from him, and he didn't follow me. I figured that ended the discussion, and, with it, my share in Steve's tennis.

That's how wrong a guy can be. About a week later, I looked at the pairings for the next bracket in the city finals, and there it was in black and white. Steven Kennedy *vs* William Wheelock. I looked again, and it was still there. Steve and I, matched against each other. Lady Luck must have had a good laugh over that one. For a minute, I was tempted to default, and then I knew darned well that I wouldn't and I knew why.

That was one match I was going to win. For just once in his life, Steve was going to be on the losing end, and it would be the best thing that could happen to him.

That match was going to be mine. It had to be.

The weather was almost perfect. My racket felt good in my hand, and in the knock-up the ball did what I wanted it to. I looked across the net at Steve. His jaw was stubborn, but his stroking was easy and cool.

I thought of everything I knew about his game. I knew, for instance, that Steve's game was primarily fast, and that anything I could do to slow him up would put him off stride. I knew that his control of a low slice to his backhand was less than perfect. I knew that I could only handle his cannonball serves by just getting them into play as deep as possible. I knew he hit more effectively on the run than standing still. I knew a lot. The problem was to use it.

Steve won the toss and went back to serve. I waited a little left of center so I could take the ball on the strong side, without having to run around it. I knew it would be deep and fast and, on the first serve, probably flat. Knowing so much about Steve gave me confidence.

The ball came over like a bullet. I took it on a late rise and sent it back, and he angled the return cross-

court. I got it back, slow-ball and spinning. He had to
wait for it, set—a shot that he hates. Slow him down,
Bill, I said to myself. Let him make errors. He's not
Superman; he'll make 'em.

He didn't on that exchange of shots, or in that game.
He took it before it went to deuce, but by that time I
knew something else. I knew that Steve was sore at me,
and that he was out to wipe up the court with me for
a mop. Being mad wasn't going to do the Kennedy
game any good at all.

I played it safe on my own serve. Long and con-
trolled; then soft spin returns, waiting for a break and
making things aggravating for my opponent. I lobbed
to his right court, knowing he'd have the sun in his eyes
when he watched the ball come down. I sliced to his
backhand whenever I had an opening. I did everything I could to keep him out of volleying position.

Steve took that first set, but it was 6-4 and I felt
pretty good. He was doing the work, and I was making
the trouble.

In the second set, he tried too hard. I knew the symptoms. He rushed the net, sent his drives a little too
long, and killed his shots. I played pat ball, and that
jammed up his control. He got madder and madder,
but he got mad at me instead of at the ball. I forced the
games to deuce on the set and prayed for luck.

Luck came my way. I took set point on a break return that tagged the cord and stumbled over. Once, in
the third set, Steve double-faulted—something he
never did. I felt satisfaction, good and deep.

I rode the ball every second. I played each point for
safety, never trying a kill or a cannonball. I took the

third set, and I earned it. It was a good thing that ten-minute rest between sets came when it did, or I'd have fallen flat on my face. But Steve didn't know that.

When we went back on the court, I opened service. My jaws ached from the way I'd set my teeth on each shot. My shoulders were sore. Steve kept wetting his lips, and I knew he was nervous, but he salted his game down, made fewer errors, and the rallies began to stretch out.

I got tireder and tireder, and my racket felt heavy in my hand. The games went endlessly to deuce, then the set, Steve pulled it out at 9-7, and his mouth was a hard, tight line.

Two sets all. The last set dragged. It pulled out like a ball of wool being unraveled. I got the works, but I kept on coming. Steve's normally fast pace was being slowed by back-spin and over-spin on my returns, and I was willing to play it that way until the well-known end of time. Then he aced me twice on serves—the ball stung past, and my eyes ached from trying to tail it. And that gave him a 4-3 lead.

I leaned over my racket for a second, getting my breath, and when I straightened up I could feel the muscles crawl in my back. I knew then that, unless the match ended pretty quick, I couldn't hold out.

I managed to take the next game, and it was 4-all. Steve started gambling on sudden-death shots, and some of them I got back to him. Don't ask me how. I had a racket in my hand and, when the ball came blazing at me, I shoveled it back. We pulled up even at deuce, and then he cracked down and took his two points and that gave him 5-4 on the set.

This could be match game, and all his, but it wasn't going to be. Not if Bill Wheelock had anything to say.

Steve was serving, and he took the first point. My wrist ached so that the racket turned in my hand as the ball struck. He took the next two points after a blistering fight—40-love.

I sent his next serve back, overloaded with spin. He swung at air—40-15, and my hopes took a leap. Steve Kennedy, missing one cold! He must be very close to folding up, and, because he was close, I felt the sudden, welcome surge of second wind. Even my racket was lighter.

On the next rally, I misjudged his drive and was caught out of position, but I reached it and played a slow shot for time to recover. Steve volleyed, unexpectedly, and I rushed the net, operating on instinct. I flung the head of my racket up, and the strings twanged. I felt the ball slide off the face and knew that it had dropped, safe, in Steve's court.

And at the same second I felt something else. I felt the tennis net against my knee. It was a fault; I'd come in too fast. Steve's game, then. Steve's match. Period.

I just stood there, with my racket hanging, knowing I'd lost. Then I heard the umpire say, "40-30," and I shook my head in a vague way, irritated because he'd got it wrong. There was a spatter of applause from the gallery, and I waited for the umpire to correct himself. He didn't.

And all of a sudden, I realized what had happened. The umpire hadn't seen the fault, and he'd awarded the point to me. I opened my mouth to say something, and then I closed it again.

Why not just let it go at that? Nobody need ever know I'd faulted. I had a chance again—a good chance. I'd got my second wind, and, if we went to deuce, Steve could never pull the game out.

I turned and walked back to the baseline.

Steve served. It was the worst service I'd ever seen come off his racket. No snap at all. I could place my drive where he'd never reach it.

I swung my racket. The ball came at me. And, all of a sudden, I knew I had everything figured wrong. I didn't want a point that I hadn't earned.

I smashed down on the ball and deliberately drove it into the net.

"Game, set and match to Kennedy," the umpire said.

I walked to the net slowly. I said, "Congratulations, Steve." He was the winner again. I'd wanted to show him something, and I just hadn't had the stuff. That was that.

Steve held out his hand, and I touched it and pulled my own away.

Steve grabbed it, good and tight. He stood there, holding onto it, and after a second I looked at him.

He said, "Any time you want to give me a good swift kick, Bill, you're welcome."

I stared.

He said, talking fast, "I saw that fault. I saw the net move when your knee touched it."

I said, "Oh." A very snappy remark.

He went on. "I know why you socked that drive into the net, after the umpire gave you the point. You didn't want to win when it wasn't legal."

This time I didn't say anything—an even snappier remark.

Steve said, "I just want to say that I've been a chump. I thought it was a lot of big talk you were making about a champion being able to lose. I didn't think you were on the level. I'm one of those guys who want proof on everything. Well, I got it." He said it again. "I've been a chump."

You could change one letter in that word and get the right answer. I said so, and then the fellows from the gallery came flocking around, wanting to congratulate the winner.

I stepped back, with a grin hanging from both ears. They had the right guy.

THE END